絵は、世界を変えられる。

時は江戸中期。表現者たちの多くが幕府によって自由を奪われていた時代――。
その圧政に筆で抗い、世界を変えた一人の男がいた。天才絵師、葛飾北斎である。
平均寿命が40年といわれた時代に、90歳で没するその日まで筆を握り続けた北斎。その不屈の男が、齢70を超え、さらなる画境を見せつけた大作こそが、かの『冨嶽三十六景』である。マネ、モネ、ゴッホ、ゴーギャンといった名だたる画家たち、さらには作曲家のドビュッシーにいたるまで、世界中のあらゆるアーティストの脳髄を刺激し、影響を与え続けた“あの波”。
およそ200年経った今もなお、色褪せることなく人々の心を掴んで離さない“あの波”が持つ、真の意味とは？
これは、自由を求め、闘い続けた男の知られざる物語である。

「絵ってなぁ、世の中変えられる」

蔦屋重三郎

Tsutaya Juzaburo

阿部 寛

ABE Hiroshi

絵や本の版元であり、販売もしている耕書堂の店主。北斎、歌麿、写楽など、江戸を熱狂させる絵師を続々と育て輩出した、当代きってのプロデューサー。早くから北斎の才能を見抜き、気にかけている。

"Paintings can change the world."

The influential publisher and owner of Tsutaya Bookshop who actively promoted the most popular artistic talents in Edo at the time, such as Hokusai, Utamaro and Sharaku. Took an early interest in Hokusai's potential.

「描きてえと思ったもんを、好きに描くだけだ」

葛飾北斎（青年期・壮年期／老年期）

Katsushika Hokusai (As a young man · In middle age / In old age)

柳楽優弥 ／ 田中 泯

YAGIRA Yuya / **TANAKA Min**

自らを画狂人と呼び、絵に全てを捧げた天才絵師。若き日に苦悩を重ねるが、苦心の末、開眼。圧倒的な画力と唯一無二の創造性でヒット作を量産。芸術家が抑圧される中、筆で抗い続けた不屈の革命家。

"I just paint what I want to paint."

A self-professed "eccentric" completely consumed by art. Perseverance through hardship as a young man framed his self-discovery and eventual development into a prolific artist of staggering talent and unparalleled creativity. A relentless revolutionary who fought against the government's oppression just with his paintbrush.

STAFF

監督：橋本 一

Director: HASHIMOTO Hajime

企画・脚本：河原れん

Chief Architect / Screenwriter: KAWAHARA Len

コト
Koto

瀧本美織
TAKIMOTO Miori

絵の道に生きる北斎を陰ながら支えた良妻。

A devoted wife who quietly supported Hokusai's artistic destiny.

高井鴻山
Takai Kozan

青木崇高
AOKI Munetaka

小布施（長野県）の豪商で、北斎の高弟。若い頃、江戸へ遊学し北斎に学ぶ。その後、小布施に帰り、北斎を招いた。

A wealthy merchant from Obuse (Nagano Prefecture) and Hokusai's leading disciple. He came to Edo as a young man to study under Hokusai. Later, he returned to Obuse and invited Hokusai to visit him.

「おめえの描く女には色気がねぇ」

喜多川歌麿
Kitagawa Utamaro

玉木 宏
TAMAKI Hiroshi

江戸中に名を馳せた美人画の大家。常に最高の美を追い求める歌麿の能力を最大限引き出すべく、重三郎は金を出して遊郭に住まわせている。表情や構図など、独自の表現方法で人気を博す。

"The women you paint have no sex appeal."

The famous painter known throughout Edo for his renderings depicting the beauty of women. Utamaro lived in the red-light district sponsored by Juzaburo, who hoped to capitalize on Utamaro's talent and relentless pursuit of ultimate beauty. His unique ability to capture facial expressions and frame a composition made his paintings immensely popular.

「筆を取るか、それとも折るか」

柳亭種彦
Ryutei Tanehiko

永山瑛太
NAGAYAMA Eita

武士の家系でありながら文才に溢れ、剣よりも筆を好んだ戯作者。北斎とは幾度もタッグを組んでいる盟友。芸術を取り締まる立場でありながら身分を隠し、強い信念を持って作品を作り続けた。

"To write or not?"

A samurai with great literary talent, who preferred writing brushes to swords. Frequently collaborated with Hokusai who illustrated his novels. While tasked by the Shogunate to crack down on rogue artists, he secretly continued to write under a pseudonym.

チーム蔦屋 PUBLISHER TSUTAYA

人気絵師を育てる名プロデューサー

Influential publisher and promoter of popular artists

蔦屋重三郎
Tsutaya Juzaburo
阿部 寛 ABE Hiroshi

恩義
Obligation

気にかけている
Interest

江戸中にその名を轟かせた花魁

Courtesan who made her name in Edo

麻雪 Asayuki
芋生 悠 IMOU Haruka

モデル
Model

少年期
Childhood

密かに尊敬
Unspoken respect

嫉妬
Jealousy

美を追求した美人画の大家

Authority on depicting the beauty of women

喜多川歌麿
Kitagawa Utamaro
玉木 宏 TAMAKI Hiroshi

友情・パートナー
Friend / Collaborator

耕書堂に身を置く物書き

Novelist who lives at Tsutaya bookshop

瑣吉／(後の)滝沢馬琴
Sakichi (later) Takizawa Bakin
辻本祐樹 TSUJIMOTO Yuki

彗星の如く現れた天才

A genius who appeared out of nowhere

東洲斎写楽 Toshusai Sharaku
浦上晟周（せいしゅう） URAGAMI Seishuu

幕府 GOVERNMENT

身分を伏せて筆を取る戯作者

Novelist writing under a pseudonym

柳亭種彦 Ryutei Tanehiko

永山瑛太 NAGAYAMA Eita

幕府配下の武家組合“小普請組”組頭

Head of the samurai union under the Shogunate

永井五右衛門 Nagai Goemon

津田寛治 TSUDA Kanji

弾圧 Crackdown

弾圧
Crackdown

友情・パートナー
Friend / Collaborator

老年期
Old Age

青年期・壮年期
Adolescence・Middle Age

葛飾北斎（デビュー時の勝川春朗）

Katsushika Hokusai
(Debut name: Katsukawa Shunro)

真の絵と、自由を求め描き続けた画狂人

“An old man mad about painting” on a relentless quest for artistic truth and freedom

葛飾北斎 | （少年期）城 桧吏（かいり）

（Childhood）JO Kairi

（青年期・壮年期）柳楽優弥

（Adolescence・Middle Age）

YAGIRA Yuya

（老年期）田中 泯

（Old Age）TANAKA Min

北斎一家 HOKUSAI FAMILY

夫婦
Wife

親子・師弟
Daughter / Pupil

北斎を支える良妻

Hokusai's supportive wife

コト Koto

瀧本美織 TAKIMOTO Miori

師弟
Disciple

父譲りの才能を秘めた娘

Hokusai's daughter who inherited his talent

お栄（応為） Oei (Oi)

河原れん KAWAHARA Len

酒造で財を成した高井家の跡取り

Heir to the Takai family who made a fortune by brewing sake

高井鴻山 Takai Kozan

青木崇高 AOKI Munetaka

画風で見る北斎年表

や狂歌絵本の挿絵、ほっそりした美人画、肉筆画や錦絵などを手掛け幅広く活躍。1798 年には琳派を抜け、北斎辰政（ときまさ）と改名する。

江島春望
早くも“あの波”の片鱗？

勝川春朗時代

勝川春章に弟子入り。入門1年目で異例の大抜擢！勝川春朗と号し、その画力を存分に発揮する。役者絵や黄表紙［きびょうし］の挿絵、さらに子供絵、おもちゃ絵、武者絵、名所絵、角力［すもう］絵、宗教画など幅広い題材の作品も発表。

四代目岩井半四郎
かしく
すみだ北斎美術館蔵

age45-52	age35-44	age19-34	age0-18
1804-1811	1794-1803	1778-1793	1760-1777

画というジャンルを開拓する。そのほかに、「百物語 さらやしき」などの幽霊画、すごろくなどの玩具画など、相変わらず幅広いジャンルを描く。

牡丹に胡蝶

絵手本の時代

全国の弟子たちのため、絵手本をおさめた「北斎漫画」が誕生。工芸品の図案集としても使われている。この時期、観客に向けた見世物として 120 畳大の巨大ダルマを描いたり、米粒に雀を 2 羽描くなどのパフォーマンスも。

北斎漫画 三編
すみだ北斎美術館蔵

読本挿絵と肉筆画 葛飾北斎時代

寛政の改革による出版規制が激化するなか、比較的規制の緩かった読本の人気が上昇。その波にのり北斎は10年間で190冊、1400点以上の挿絵を描いた。滝沢馬琴、柳亭種彦ともこの頃からタッグを組み始める。

阿波濃鳴門
国文学研究資料館蔵
柳亭種彦との初タッグ作。

琳派・俵屋宗理、北斎辰政時代

勝川派を抜けた後、琳派に入門し、俵屋宗理2代目を襲名。勝川派、琳派とも異なる自由で大胆な構図で独自の宗理様式を確立した。摺物［すりもの］

風流無くてなゝくせ
遠眼鏡
山口県立萩美術館・
浦上記念館蔵

あの波が誕生！

age75-90
1834-1849

age71-74
1830-1833

age53-70
1812-1829

晩年期 肉筆画の時代

晩年は肉筆画に傾倒し、題材も風俗画から和漢の故事に則した作品や宗教画、自然を題材にしたものへと大きく変化し、写実を追求した重厚感のある画風へと変化していく。1849年春、浅草にて90年の生涯を終える。

女浪 北斎館蔵

男浪 北斎館蔵

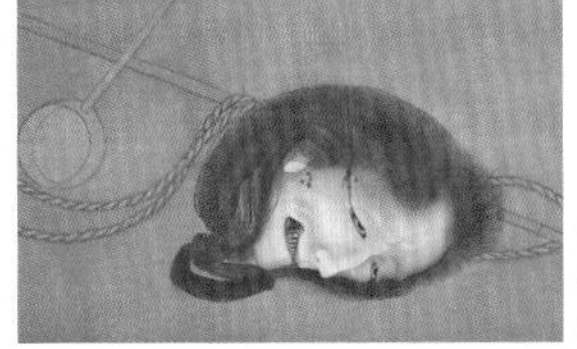

生首の図
種彦の死と同時期に描かれた。

錦絵の時代

花鳥画や錦絵の名作を多数生み出す。当時流行の富士信仰の波にのって大ヒットした「冨嶽三十六景」により、もともと浮世絵に存在しなかった風景

冨嶽三十六景
神奈川沖浪裏

年表の英訳は本の後ろから2～3ページ目にあります。
The English translation of the chronology is on the second and third pages from the back of the book.

“Paintings can change the world.”

Mid-18th century Edo period, Japan
In an era when the Shogunate government stifled the creative freedom of many artists, one man railed against the oppression and changed the world only with his paintbrush – the genius, Katsushika Hokusai.
While the average lifespan at the time was 40 years, Hokusai continued to paint until the day he died at the age of 90. Even after completing his masterpiece, “Thirty-six Views of Mt. Fuji” well into his 70’s, Hokusai had yet more to give and dimensions to explore. His “Wave” has influenced and stimulated artists around the world from master painters such as Manet, Monet, Van Gogh and Gauguin, to the composer Debussy.
What is the true meaning of the “Wave” -- a timeless image that to this day never ceases to captivate the hearts of all who see it, even after 200 years?
This drama is the untold story of a man and his unyielding quest for freedom.

シナリオブック

もくじ

1A　道

焼けつくような陽光の下。汗だくで棒切れを動かし、地面に絵を描く北斎（幼年期・十歳前後）。

そこへ、悪童たちが集まり、意地悪く北斎の絵を踏みにじる。

キッと睨（にら）みつける北斎。悪童たちに跳びかかるが、あっという間に押し倒され、乱暴に殴られる。

押し潰（つぶ）されながらも、猛々（たけだけ）しい目つきで、何度も立ち上がろうともがく北斎。

1B　妓楼（ぎろう）の一室

蝋燭（ろうそく）の灯りに照らされながら、遊女（ゆうじょ）と向き合い、絵を描く北斎（青年期）。遊女は、全裸のしどけない姿でポーズを取るが、北斎は、むしろ自分のイマジネーションに興奮するがごとく、汗を光らせ、夢中で絵筆を走らせる。

1C　北斎の工房兼自宅

なだれこむような豪雨が、古びた工房の軒先に打ちつけている。
思わず工房から走り出てくる、北斎（老年期）。
両手のひらに載せられたベロ藍の絵の具を、天に掲げる。
雨を受け、溶けるベロ藍……。
真っ青な奔流が、北斎を染め上げていく。
その姿にかぶさって――

タイトル　鮮やかに「HOKUSAI」

2　北斎の家（長屋）・外観

生活感に溢れた、裏路地。泥と汚物に満ちている。

3　同・内

薄暗い部屋の中には、北斎がこれまで描いてきた絵が乱雑に並んでいる。
勝川派、狩野派、唐絵、西洋画の習作、写生帖……。
その部屋の片隅で、牡丹を描く北斎（青年期）。
若々しく、どこかがむしゃらな、その筆致。

字幕「壱の章」

4　江戸の書店・蔦屋耕書堂・外

富士紋を抜かれた暖簾が翻る。
そこへ。客を押しのけ、与力を筆頭とした役人たちが押し入っていく。

与力「御用改めである！」

騒然とする店内。土足で踏みにじられる、浮世絵や書籍。客が押し出され、手代たちが突き飛ばされる。

5 同・内

与力「耕書堂主人、蔦屋重三郎！」

居丈高な役人に相対し、飄々と構える男――この店の主人、蔦屋重三郎である。心配そうに成行きを見守る妻・トヨと瑣吉（後の馬琴）たち使用人。

重三郎「――」

与力「その方、ご禁制を犯し、みだりに洒落本開版し風俗を書き著したる、重々不届きにつき、身上半減の闕所申し付けるものなり！」

言ったそばから、役人たちが、一斉に店内の商品などを外に放り出し、火にくべる。騒ぎの中、富士紋の暖簾が落ち、チリチリと火が回る。

重三郎「……！」

険しい目で役人を見る重三郎。役人も負けじと睨み返すが、気圧され、わずかに怯む。破壊の狂乱。版木や絵も次々と燃やされる中、重三郎は、静かに怒りをたぎらせる。

重三郎「……（耐えて）」

6　北斎の家・内

長屋の薄い壁から響く、両隣の嬌声(きょうせい)や生活音。
それを意にも介さず、黙々と絵の具を溶く北斎。

7　蔦屋耕書堂・店前〜内

役人たちによって滅茶苦茶にされた店。
箒(ほうき)を手にしたトヨが気丈に片付けを始めている。それに続く、番頭(ばんとう)、使用人たち。
すすの中から、喜多川歌麿(きたがわうたまろ)の絵を拾い上げる瑣吉。
と。重三郎、横からそれを取り、汚れを袖で払い落としつつ、

重三郎「こんなに汚れちまっても、ちっとも色気を失っちゃいねえ。さすがは歌麿だ」
瑣吉「ええ」
重三郎「……まったく、ありがてえもんだ」
瑣吉「（顔を上げ）？」

重三郎　「出る杭は打たれるってな。つまり、うちが江戸で頭ひとつ抜けた版元だって、お墨付きをもらえたってこった」
　　　と、微かに笑む。
トヨ　「……」
瑣吉　「……」
重三郎　「（店を見回し）江戸一の絵師、戯作者。どれも俺が育ててきた奴らだ。まったく面白え。こいつぁ、恵みの雨ってもんよ」
瑣吉　「……」
重三郎　「これで、江戸中がうちの出方に目ェ凝らしやがる。種を植えるには、またとない折ってことよ」

8　北斎の家

　　　鮮やかに絵を描き上げる北斎。
　　　その表情……。

9　吉原・大門通り（夜）

華やかな通りを悠々と歩いていく重三郎。

10　美乃屋・帳場〜座敷

吉原の妓楼（重三郎の実家）。
入ってくる重三郎のもとへ、楼主がやってくる。
源次郎——重三郎の義弟である。

源次郎「兄さん！」
重三郎「（笑って）忙しそうだな」
源次郎「（も、笑み）どうにかな」
重三郎「やっと商売が板についてきたじゃねえか。親父の面影が見えるようだよ」
源次郎「よせやい。まだまだ足元にも及ばねえ。今だって客のイザコザでてんやわんやだ」
重三郎「ここは毎晩が祭だからな」

奥からドドンと、喧嘩の音。

源次郎　「（舌打ちして）芋侍どもが」

重三郎　「侍も商人も、同じ男よ。ここに来りゃあ箍が外れる」

×　×　×

階段を上がり、廊下を行く二人。重三郎の手には銚子がある。

襖越しに三味線の音。女郎の笑い声。

奥座敷の前で足を止める重三郎。

スッと襖を開ける。

重三郎　「……」

毛氈上の紙を前に座する、喜多川歌麿。

恍惚とした表情で、女絵を描いている。

傍らには、半裸姿のモデル役の女郎が、うっとりとした表情で横たわっている。

重三郎。気付かせるように中に入り、銚子を畳に置く。

歌麿　「（見て）……」

顎をしゃくる。

文机の上。数枚の絵が仕上がっている。

重三郎　「（満足げな表情で）」

絵を受け取り、出ていこうとすると、

歌麿　「錦屋にな。麻雪(あさゆき)っていう花魁(おいらん)がいるらしい」

重三郎　「（振り返り）」

歌麿　「いい目をしてると、耳にしてね」

重三郎　「（頷き）おめえさんが言うなら、京女だって江戸に呼ぶよ」

歌麿　「……」

出ていく重三郎。

11　錦屋・内

キセルをふかし、胡乱(うろん)な目で重三郎を見る麻雪。

麻雪　「嫌でありんす」

重三郎　「……どうしてだ？　悪ィ話じゃねえはずだ」

麻雪　「わちきは絵師が、嫌いでありんす」

重三郎　「……（理由を目で問う）」

麻雪　「礼儀ってもんがないからね。こないだなんて、一晩中、わちきを立たせたヤツがいた」

重三郎　「……ずいぶん、ご熱心なヤツじゃねえか」

麻雪　「（フンと鼻で嗤い）冗談じゃない。あれは、行儀を知らねえ山猿みてえなヤツさ。やれ、いい線が出ねえだのなんの、わちきに覆いかぶさるようにして描きやがった」

重三郎　「（笑って）さぞかし、いい絵ができたろうな」

麻雪　「そりゃそうさ、わちきを描いたんだもの――でも、もう二度とごめんだね」

麻雪、煙を吐き、

麻雪　「山猿の前に立つのはさ」

12　蔦屋耕書堂・内（翌日）

瑣吉、「あぁ」と合点し、大きく頷く。

瑣吉　「それなら間違いねえや。春朗ですよ。勝川春朗」

重三郎　「勝川？」

瑣吉　「へぇ。ウチでも何枚か描かせてますよ。（笑い）山猿とは全く、言い得て妙だ」

と、絵を探しにいき、『春朗』名で描かれた北斎の絵をいくつか持ってくる。

重三郎、受け取り、

重三郎「(見て)……」

瑣吉「腕は悪かねえんだが。ただ、描きたくねえもんは描かねえ。描くなら気が済むまでって、何かと七面倒くさいヤツでして……」

重三郎「(やや興味を惹かれ)」

瑣吉「今はどうしてんのか知りませんが」

重三郎「勝川にはいないのか?」

瑣吉「とっくに。破門されちまって」

重三郎「……破門?」

13 寺の境内

絵を売る北斎。その姿に——

瑣吉の声「絵となると見境がなくなるヤツなんですよ。勝川にいながら大和絵を描くは、狩野にも足を突っ込んじまうは。しまいには兄弟子を殴っちまったそうで」

重三郎の声　「殴った？　なんでまた……」
瑣吉の声　「さあ」
道行く人は、無骨な態度で絵を売る北斎に見向きもしない。
北斎、諦めたような、倦んだ表情で、ボンヤリと……。

14　北斎の家・外

隣家の悪童と、叱りつける母親の声が響いている。
そこへ、帰ってきた北斎。
戸を開けようとして、誰かの気配を感じて――
北斎　「……？」

15　同・内

怪訝そうに入ってくる北斎。
勝手に家に上がり、絵を見比べる男の姿。

男、振り返る――重三郎である。

北斎　「！　あんた……」

重三郎　「……」

北斎　「耕書堂の」

重三郎　「……ちょっと絵を拝見したくてな。なかなか帰ってこねえから勝手に上がらせてもらったよ」

北斎　「……なんの用だ？」

重三郎　「ちゃんと生きてるかってな」

北斎　「？」

重三郎　「うちの瑣吉が言ってたぜ」

北斎　「……」

重三郎　「おめえさん、食えてんのか？」

北斎　「……大きなお世話だ」

重三郎　「……」

北斎　「……時々、絵を売ってしのいでいる」

重三郎　「絵を？」

北斎　「（一瞬、表情陰るが）あぁ」

重三郎　「金になるのか」

北斎　「まぁな」

重三郎、手にしていた絵をポンと無下に置き、

重三郎　「おめえ。うちで描いてみる気はねえか？」

北斎　「（微かに表情が強張る）」

重三郎　「俺が一から育ててやる」

北斎　「……」

重三郎　「どうした？」

北斎　「……断る」

重三郎　「（意外な言葉に驚き）？」

北斎　「悪いが、俺は人の指図で仕事すんのは、どうも性に合わねえ」

重三郎　「（しばし考え）……なるほど」

北斎　「……？」

重三郎　「おめえ、兄弟子を殴ったんだってな」

北斎　「それも瑣吉の野郎か？」

重三郎　「（頷き）あぁ。なぜ殴った？」

北斎　「……絵に筆を入れられたからだ」

重三郎　「……」

北斎　「俺の絵が台無しになっちまった」

重三郎、微かに笑み、

重三郎　「そうか。邪魔したな」

と、戸口へ向かう。

北斎　「（その背中を見送り）……」

16　寺の境内（日替わり）

同じ場所に、絵を並べて売る北斎。

いっこうに客は来ず——

北斎　「……」

17　北斎の家

帰ってくる北斎。
戸を開けると蔦屋の紋が入った紙包みがあり、

北斎「……」
開くと、金が入っている。

18　蔦屋耕書堂・内

不快そうな顔でやってくる北斎。
店番をしながら原稿を書いていた瑣吉。
顔を上げ、

瑣吉「……」
やっぱり来たか、と北斎を見る。

瑣吉「久しぶりだな」

北斎「……」

瑣吉「（笑み）旦那様かい？」

北斎「（頷く）」

瑣吉「吉原（よしわら）だよ」

19　美乃屋・外（夜）

やってくる北斎。

20　同・廊下

男衆（おとこし）に案内されて、廊下を行く北斎。

21　同・奥座敷

バン！と襖（ふすま）を開ける北斎。と。

麻雪をモデルに絵を描く歌麿の姿が、目に飛び込んでくる。

面食らう北斎。

歌麿　「（も、驚いて見る）……」

麻雪は、北斎を冷たく睨（にら）んで。

麻雪　「……」

重三郎　「（わざとらしく）これはこれは……。面白い男がやってきた」

歌麿　「知り合いか？」

重三郎　「あぁ。たまさか見つけた絵師よ」

麻雪　「（かぶせて）——猿でありんす」

歌麿。麻雪の言い方で合点し、

歌麿　「あぁ、コイツが噂の勝川春朗か」

重三郎　「もう、勝川ではないがな」

北斎　「……」

重三郎　「ま、そんなとこに突っ立ってないで、座ったらどうだ？　歌麿先生が吉原一の花を描くところだ」

プイと横を向く麻雪。

北斎も、突っ立ったまま、憮然とする。

北斎　「……」

歌麿　「俺ァ別に構わねえが。まぁ。せっかく来たんだ。おめえも……どうだ、一杯？」

と、北斎に向けて銚子(ちょうし)を上げる。が、

北斎　「酒は飲まん」

居心地悪く、睨(にら)む北斎。

歌麿、笑って。

歌麿　「そりゃ、けっこうだ。コイツなら酒代払わんでも、ガッポリ稼いでくれるぞ」

重三郎　「……（含み笑い）」

北斎　「……」

歌麿　「いいから座れや。うめえ魚があるぜ。おめえさんも食ってけや」

北斎　「贅沢なもんは口に合わん」

歌麿、呵々(かか)と笑って、

歌麿　「（重三郎に）聞いたか？　こいつ、本当に絵師なのか？」

重三郎　「そのようだ」

歌麿　「まるで、坊さんみてえな野郎だな。だから、女に色気がねえんだ」

北斎　「？」

歌麿　「おめえの描く女には色気がねえ」

北斎　「……（カチン）」

歌麿　「なぁ、蔦屋」

重三郎　「……」

北斎を横目で見る麻雪。

歌麿　「下手だとは言わねえよ。ただ。そうだな。てめえの絵は目の前にあるものを似せて描いただけの絵だ」

歌麿。御膳にのった魚のお頭（かしら）を指し、

歌麿　「上っ面だけで、命が見えねえ」

北斎　「……」

みるみる、血が上（のぼ）っていく。

重三郎　「（その表情を見ている）」

北斎。いたたまれず、憤然と踵（きびす）を返すと、

重三郎　「おい」

北斎を止める。

重三郎　「逃げるのか?」
北斎　「……」
重三郎　「おめえだけじゃねえぞ」
北斎　「?」
重三郎　「絵師など、ほかにいくらでもいる」
北斎　「……」
歌麿　「……」
その物言いに、歌麿、
歌麿　「悪いが、そこ、閉めてくれるか」
北斎　「?」
北斎、一瞬たじろぐが、目つきを変えた歌麿に気圧され、襖（ふすま）を閉め、座る。
二人の絵師を眺める重三郎。
歌麿、今まで描いていた絵を、グシャグシャッと丸め、
歌麿　「（麻雪に）さて。麻雪殿には……」
麻雪　「（色っぽく顔を上げ）?」
歌麿、筆を取り、

歌麿　「後ろを向いて座ってくれ」

麻雪　「……（言われるまま）」

歌麿、その様子を眺めつつ、麻雪のうなじの辺りを撫でるようになぞり……着物の襟を大胆に開く。

麻雪　「（抵抗する暇もなく）！」

襟を大きく寛げたポーズ。

歌麿　「鏡を持ってくれるか？」

麻雪、鏡に自分を映す。立ち上る色香。

歌麿の目にも妖気が宿る。

間。

やがて柔らかく筆を構えると、サラサラと描き始める歌麿。流れるような線。麻雪をほとんど見ることもなく、描きつけていく。

北斎　「……」

22　蔦屋耕書堂・内（翌日）

原稿を書いている瑣吉。気配に目を上げると、北斎が立っている。

瑣吉　「（顔を上げ）おぉ、春（朗）……」

北斎　「……」

瑣吉を憮然と見下ろす北斎。

北斎　「……歌麿は、いつもあそこに住んでるのか？」

瑣吉　「そうだよ。食うも寝るも絵を描くのも、みんなあの座敷だ」

北斎　「……」

瑣吉　「勘定は、全部うちさ。べらぼうな額だぜ」

北斎　「なら、出さなきゃいいじゃねえか」

瑣吉　「（苦笑して）あそこに住まわせたのは、旦那様の方だ。絵を描かせるために、女漬けにしたのさ」

北斎　「（驚く）」

瑣吉　「おかげで店は火の車だ。お上(かみ)に店の金をあらかた持ってかれちまったってのによ。

北斎　（ボソリと）たまんねえよな。こっちは読んでさえもらえねえのに」

北斎　「？」

　　　琑吉の原稿——

　　　何度も書き直した跡がある。

琑吉　「で。おめえさんはどうすんで？　絵は描くのか？」

北斎　「（曖昧に）いや……そうだ。これ（と金の入った包みを渡す）」

琑吉　「？」

北斎　「返しといてくれ。うちに置いてきやがったが、受け取れねえ」

琑吉　「旦那様が？」

北斎　「あぁ」

琑吉　「……じゃあ、描かねえつもりか？」

北斎　「……」

23　北斎の家

　　　黙々と女絵を描く北斎。

筆を走らせ、女の表情を描いていく。

24　蔦屋耕書堂・奥座敷

やや緊張の面持ちで、４枚の女絵（『風流無くてなゝくせ』）を並べる北斎。

重三郎（体調が崩れてきている）が対座し、絵を見る。

同席する瑣吉、そのうまさに驚くが、

重三郎「……」

重三郎は、落胆の色を浮かべる。

重三郎「どういうつもりだ」

北斎「どうって」

瑣吉「（重三郎を？と見る）」

北斎「よく見てみろよ。歌麿よりもうめえじゃねえか！」

重三郎「おめえは、勝ち負けで絵を描いてんのか？」

北斎「……」

重三郎「おめえ、なんで絵を描いている？」

北斎　「何の話だ？」

重三郎　「言葉のとおりだ。なぜ絵を描いている？」

北斎　「……ンなの、分かんねえよ」

重三郎　「……」

北斎　「……俺は、たいした家の生まれじゃねえ。口減らしで、三つの時に丁稚に出された。生きていくのがやっとってとこだ」

重三郎　「で、なぜ絵師になったんだ」

北斎　「絵なら下っ端から這い上がれると思ってな。絵を描くのに身分は関係ないだろ。うまけりゃいくらだって上に……（這い上がれる）」

重三郎　「（吐き捨てるように）なら、やめろ」

北斎　「？」

重三郎　「やめちまえ。そんな屁みてえなことにこだわってんなら」

北斎　「なんだと？」

重三郎　「……」

重三郎、いくばくかの金を投げ置いて立ち去る。
呆気にとられる北斎。

北斎　「（悔しく）なんだよ」
瑣吉　「……」
北斎　「チキショウが！」

憤る北斎。
絵も金も置いたまま出ていく。

25　美乃屋・奥座敷（夜）

銚子（ちょうし）や画材が散乱した床。
麻雪を抱く歌麿。
恍惚（こうこつ）としながらも、観察するような眼差しで、麻雪の肢体（したい）の曲線をなぞっていく。

26　北斎の家（日替わり・昼〜夜）

描く北斎。隣家の音は、相変わらず喧（かまびす）しい。
部屋には、方向が定まらず、試行錯誤で描いた絵が、山と散乱している。

北斎「（ついに筆が止まって）……」
手を下ろす。
じっと紙を見つめ続ける北斎。

27　蔦屋耕書堂・内

店先。病から、わずかに虚ろな表情を見せる、重三郎。
その横顔を心配そうに覗くトヨ。
そこへ、源次郎が興奮気味に飛び込んでくる。
源次郎「兄さん！」
重三郎「？」
×　×　×
風呂敷から絵を取り出す源次郎。
絵を見る重三郎。その顔、みるみる驚きに満ちていく。
重三郎「誰の絵だ？」
源次郎。重三郎の驚きに、期待どおりと笑って、

源次郎　「実は、うちの客なんだ。まだ若ぇんだが、遊び方まで心得ているヤツでよぉ」
重三郎　「……」
源次郎　「道楽で絵を描いてんだが、こいつがなかなかのもんなんだ。兄さんなら、絶対分かると思ったよ」
重三郎　「（頷き）」
源次郎　「描くのは歌舞伎の役者絵だけだ。芝居を観にいっては、戯れに描いたというが……」
重三郎　「……」
源次郎　「単なるおふざけには見えねえ」
重三郎　「（絵に引き寄せられて）――会えるか？」
源次郎　「もちろんだ。絵は、ほかにもまだあるらしいぜ」
重三郎　「（興奮して）よし、うちで買い取ろう。全部だ。全部、うちが買う！」

28　北斎の家・外

井戸水をバシャンとかぶる北斎。

手の汗が止まらず、何度も手を擦り合わせる。

北斎　「（情けなく）……」

唸り声を上げる。

29　美乃屋・重三郎の座敷（夜）

源次郎に案内され、東洲斎写楽（とうしゅうさいしゃらく）がやってくる。顔立ちにはまだ少年のような若さが残るが、洒落た着物をさらりと着こなしている。

一礼する写楽。重三郎、大げさに歓迎して、

重三郎　「耕書堂の主、蔦屋重三郎でございます」

写楽　「（微笑む）御高名はかねがね」

重三郎　「さ、どうぞ」

30　北斎の家

半裸で、美人画を仕上げている北斎。

31 美乃屋・重三郎の座敷

持参した絵を広げる写楽。
目を輝かせて見入る重三郎。
写楽。重三郎の前で筆を取り、悠々と絵を描いていく。

32 北斎の家

苦闘の末――絵を描き上げた北斎。

33 蔦屋耕書堂・工房（日替わり）

店に隣接した工房。
土気色の顔をした重三郎が、精気を絞り出すようにしながら、刷り上がったばかりの写楽の絵を確認している。

重三郎　「……足んねえな」

摺師（すりし）　「……足んねえ、ですか」

重三郎　「あぁ。いっぺん見たら目に焼き付いちまうような絵にしてえんだ」

摺師、戸惑っていると。重三郎、ふいに思いつき、

重三郎　「雲母（きら）だ」

摺師　「へ？」

重三郎　「雲母摺（ずり）だ！」

摺師　「そいつァ無茶だ……。儲けが吹っ飛んじゃいますぜ」

重三郎　「（不敵な笑みを浮かべる）」

と。そこへ瑣吉が呼びにきて。

瑣吉　「旦那様！」

重三郎　「？」

34　同・廊下

客間に通され待つ北斎に、廊下から目を向ける重三郎。

風呂敷に包んだ絵を抱く北斎。
その、自信のない表情を見て、

重三郎　「（瑣吉に）帰ってもらえ」
瑣吉　「え？」
重三郎　「あの絵はいらん」
瑣吉　「しかし……」
重三郎　「（首を振り）」
引き返していく。

35　同・内〜外

肩を落とし、絵を持って出ていく北斎。
瑣吉　「（見送り）……」

36　北斎の家（日替わり）

それでもまだ描き続けようとする北斎。
虚ろな目。
絵の具もついに果てて……
北斎「……」

37　寺の境内

再び、絵を売る北斎。
絵は売れず……。

38　道

賑わう雑踏の中、歩いてくる北斎。
すると。
耕書堂の前に、人垣ができているのが見える。
北斎「?・」

近づいていくと――

39　蔦屋耕書堂・外

店先で大々的に写楽が売り出されている。

北斎「（驚いて）」

引き寄せられるように、中へと入っていく。

40　同・内

強烈なインパクトを放ち、並んでいる写楽の役者絵。

北斎。その一枚一枚を、茫然自失の表情で見ていく。

瑣吉「（気付くが）……」

声を掛けられず。

すると。奥から、通人（つうじん）仲間と話す重三郎の声が聞こえてくる。

北斎、思わず踵（きびす）を返す。

が——重三郎。瑣吉の目線の先にいる北斎に気付いて。

重三郎「(北斎に) おい」

北斎。立ち止まる。

重三郎「せっかく来たんだから、挨拶くらいしてったらどうだ」

おずおずと振り返る北斎。

周囲に陳列した写楽の絵。

上機嫌の重三郎。

北斎。何事か言おうとするが……重三郎に見据えられ、言葉を飲み込む。

重三郎「名は、東洲斎写楽という。俺が一目で惚れた絵師だ」

北斎「……」

41　美乃屋・座敷

写楽の出版を祝う宴。豪華な料理が並べられ、遊女(ゆうじょ)たちが華を添えている。

上客たちに写楽を紹介し、お酌してまわる重三郎。

重三郎「写楽先生だ。誰にも真似できねえ絵を描く。まさに奇才と呼ぶにふさわしい」

そんな中、北斎だけが、下座にポツリと仏頂面で座っている。
番頭新造(ばんとうしんぞう)がお酌に来ても、

北斎　「いらん」

と、すげなく断る。

上客1　「(重三郎の酌を受けながら)まさか、こんな若い男が、あの絵を描いたとはね。いや、にわかに信じられん」

写楽　「(笑む)」

上客2　「(重三郎に)全くあんたの目利きは舌を巻くよ」

重三郎　「いやいや。今度のは源次郎の手柄ですよ。あいつが写楽先生を見つけてくれた」

上客2　「とはいえ、おめえさんじゃなけりゃ、こんな花火は上げられんじゃろう?」

北斎　「……」

耐えるように聞いている。
そこへ。襖(ふすま)を開け、堂々、歌麿が入ってくる。

歌麿　「これはこれは、お揃いで」

合わせたように頭を下げる先客たち。少し遅れて会釈する写楽。微動だにしない北斎。

歌麿　「……」

北斎には目もくれず、上座に着く。

スッと身をかわし、歌麿の前に出て、お酌をする写楽。その姿を見つめる歌麿。

歌麿　「（写楽に）いいスジしてんな」

写楽　「？」

歌麿　「絵のことだ」

写楽　「（頭を下げる）」

歌麿　「度肝を抜かれたよ。こんな絵があるものか、とな」

三味線が鳴り、さらに入ってくる遊女（ゆうじょ）たち。最後尾には、麻雪の姿。

麻雪　「……」

重三郎と目を交わしながら、写楽の隣に座る。

麻雪　「（写楽に）この度は、おめでとうござんす」

深々と頭を下げる。

写楽と視線を交わす麻雪。二人を見る歌麿。

歌麿　「……」

その様子を、遠巻きに瑣吉が窺っている。

瑣吉　「……」

歌麿。写楽に返盃しながら、

歌麿　「ひとつ聞きてえんだが、なにかい？　おめえさんの目には役者があぁ見えるのかい？」

写楽　「あぁ、というのは？」

挑発するように、写楽の『三世大谷鬼次の奴江戸兵衛』のポーズを見せる歌麿。

写楽　「（微笑み）できるなら、この目をとってお見せしたいですが……」

歌麿　「（笑い）」

写楽　「（も、笑み）姿形を似せるだけでは、飽き足らないもので」

と、盃をあける。そつなく、写楽に銚子を傾ける麻雪。

歌麿　「……大げさに描けば、面白いと？」

写楽　「とんでもない。役者の心を映したまでですよ」

歌麿　「……」

冷たい一瞥を向け、盃をあける歌麿。麻雪の酌は断り、自分で盃を満たす。

三味線、鼓の音が高くなり、芸者が舞を披露する。

その中で、すっかり蚊帳の外に置かれた北斎。

北斎　「……」

居心地悪く、俯いている。
と。目の前の盃に溢れるほど酒が注がれ、ハッと目を上げると、重三郎が見下ろしている。

北斎　「酒は飲まんと言っただろう」

重三郎　「知っておる」

北斎　「……」

重三郎　「顔を上げさせようと思ったのだ」

北斎　「……全く、胸糞悪ィや」

重三郎を睨む北斎。

重三郎　「……」

北斎　「あれが、絵だって言うのか？　あんなもんを、あんたは探してたのか？」

重三郎　「(自信たっぷりに）あぁ」

北斎　「冗談じゃねえや！　あんなもんを描くやつは、絵師とは呼ばねえ！　顔も手も、大きさなんかデタラメじゃねえか！　顔だって、見ろ、どいつも、ひょっとこみてえな面してやがる！」

重三郎　「写楽殿は、おめえのような絵師ではないからな」
北斎　「……？」
重三郎　「どこぞやの門下に属したこともない。師匠も持たぬ」
北斎　「……なら、なんで絵が描けるんだ」
重三郎　「（写楽に視線を向ける）」
写楽　「（謙虚に笑み）ただ、道楽で描いたまでです」
北斎　「⁉」
歌麿　「……」
写楽　「いつの間にか筆を持ち、興じているうちに描くようになりまして」
北斎　「（訳が分からず）ふざけているのか？」
写楽　「？（キョトン）」
北斎　「道楽で絵が描けるもんか！」
　カッとなり、思わず膝を立てる。サッとやってきて、北斎を止める琑吉。
写楽　「（さらにキョトンとし）私はただ心の赴くままに、描くだけです」
　重三郎に向き直り、睨（にら）む北斎。
重三郎　「……」

北斎をじっと見据える。返す言葉もなく、座り込む北斎。
目を落とすと、御膳の上には、魚の頭。

北斎「……」

42　北斎の家（日替わり）

もぬけの殻となった部屋。手土産を手に佇む瑣吉。
荒れた室内には、置きっ放しの絵や割れた絵皿が散乱している。

瑣吉「……」

43　道（日替わり）

わずかばかりの荷物を背負い、歩く北斎。

44 夜道

暗闇。野宿する北斎。焚き火の明かり。
その見開かれた目。炎を見つめる。絵筆の入った矢立（やたて）を火にくべようとするが……
できない。

45 田舎道（日替わり）

行く北斎。

46 寺の山門

雨。軒先で雨宿りする北斎。
空腹だが、食べるものはない。

47　蔦屋耕書堂・廊下

縁側から雨を見上げる重三郎。
その、やつれきった横顔。
そこへトヨが来て。

トヨ「まぁ。こんな寒いところに……！」
重三郎「ん」
トヨ「お医者様がいらっしゃいましたと、先ほどから呼んでおりましたのに……」
重三郎「あぁ」
雨を見つめる重三郎。

48　白骨林の道

抜け殻のような北斎、歩いていく。気力もなく、さまようように。

49　草むら（夕）

空腹に耐えかね、雑草を口に入れる北斎。
が、あまりの不味さにむせて吐き出す。

50　美乃屋・重三郎の座敷

ひとり、ぼんやりと酒を飲む重三郎。
床に広げているのは——世界地図。

51　草むら（時間経過）

気力も体力も失せ、眠る北斎。
しばらく後、ようやく目を覚ますと……。
その耳に、遠くから波の音が聞こえてくる。

52 海

波の音に引き寄せられ、ふらふらと歩いてくる北斎。
ふと、足が止まる。
――海だ。

北斎「(目を奪われ)……」

波打ち際へと進んでいく。
寄せては返すさざ波。
水平線の先には、すっくと富士がそびえている。
何かを感じる北斎。写生帖を取り出し、筆を走らせるが、なかなかうまくいかない。

北斎「……」

夢中で何度も線を描く北斎。悔しさとイラ立ち、そして、留まることを知らない波への興味が湧いてくる。
目を閉じる北斎。波の音を聞き、海へと足を運ぶ。
足に寄せる波。その波頭を肌から感じ取っていく。

さらに進み、ザブッと海に身をつける北斎。
波の音、潮の香り……。
それら全てを体に染み込ませるように、ひたすら五感を研ぎ澄ませる。

北斎「……」

53 道

江戸の街へ戻ってくる、北斎の姿。

54 蔦屋耕書堂・寝室

病床に伏せている重三郎。
そこへ、瑣吉。

瑣吉「旦那様……」

重三郎「……？」

× × ×

家紋の入った着物に着替える重三郎。
それを手伝うトヨ。

55　蔦屋耕書堂（閉店中）・内

客はいない。一人待つ北斎。
精一杯の足取りで歩いてくる重三郎。
北斎の前に現れ、対座する。
離れたところから、見守るトヨと瑣吉。
重三郎。北斎の日に焼けた顔を見て。

重三郎　「――いい顔になったたな」

北斎　「（も、重三郎を見るが）……」
言葉がない。

重三郎　「待ちくたびれちまってな。（と、苦笑いし）江戸患（わずら）いだ。長くはねえ」
と、手を差し出す。

北斎　「……」

風呂敷を取り、絵を渡す北斎。

重三郎　「……」

波の絵。予想外の絵に、重三郎、言葉に詰まる。

北斎　「ただ描きてえと思ったもんを、好きに描いただけだ」

絵に引き込まれる重三郎。

食い入るように絵を見続ける。

北斎　「いらねえんなら、そうと言ってくれ」

重三郎　「（その自信に驚き）……」

視線を北斎に向ける。

重三郎　「波か。……面白えじゃねえか。まさか、こう来るとは思わなかったが」

北斎　「……」

重三郎　「ずいぶんな波だな。見たこともねえ形なのに、これこそ波だと語ってやがる」

北斎　「……」

再び、絵に視線を戻す重三郎。

重三郎　「いい絵だ。こいつで……」

北斎　「……」

重三郎　「うちで、一枚描いてもらえねえだろうか」
北斎　「（ハッと重三郎を見る）」
重三郎　「……」

56 美乃屋・廊下（日替わり・夜）

賑やかに、芸妓（げいこ）や客が行く。

57 同・重三郎の座敷

仕上がったばかりの『江島春望（えのしましゅんぼう）』を見る北斎と重三郎。
重三郎。満足そうに絵を眺め、水平線上に描かれた富士山を見つめる。

重三郎　「おめえ。やっと化けたな」
北斎　「……」
重三郎　「これぁ、おめえにしか描けねえ絵だ。この富士と同じ。二つとあらずと書いて『不二』。だから美しいってな」

北斎　「……」

北斎。やっと安堵の息をつく。

その背中をポンと叩く重三郎。

重三郎　「『北斎』か。名前も面白れえ」

『江島春望（えのしましゅんぼう）』。その落款（らっかん）には、『北斎宗理（そうり）』と書かれている。

北斎　「北極星にちなんで付けたんだ。たったひとつ、ぜってえに動かねえ星だ」

その言葉に、笑みを浮かべる重三郎。北斎に初めて見せる、心からの笑みだ。

重三郎。無造作に、世界地図をポンと出す。

北斎　「?」

重三郎　「広げてみろや」

言われたとおり、地図を広げる北斎。

北斎　「（見て）……」

重三郎　「江戸なんてのはな。（指でさし）そン中の、米粒よりも小っちぇえところだ。笑っちまうだろ」

北斎　「……」

重三郎　「……俺はこれ見てるとな、昔から気持ちよく酔えるんだ。余計なこたァ全部忘れて、片っ端から旅して回る」

北斎　「海の先に何があるんだ？」

重三郎　「うめぇ酒がある。食いもんも、女も、もちろん絵だって見たこともねぇもんばっかりだ。俺はな、そこで、店をやんのよ」

重三郎の目に、ふいに強い力が宿る。

重三郎　「見たこともねぇ国で、オレが見込んだ奴らの絵を売って、商いをする。オレの目には狂いがねぇってとこを見せてやんだ」

北斎　「……」

重三郎、盃を飲み干す。

重三郎　「こんなとこで、ウカウカしてられっかってな」

立ち上がる重三郎。

北斎　「……？」

重三郎　「ちぃと酒を取ってくる。今日はうめぇ酒が飲めそうだ」

と、ふらつく足取りで部屋を出ていく。
背に抜いた紋に、浮かぶ家紋の富士。

北斎　「……」

58　重三郎の葬列

蔦屋の関係者、揃いの富士家紋の半纏(はんてん)を着て、ズラリと並び歩く。位牌を持つトヨ。
瑣吉、源次郎も列をなす。

59　蔦屋耕書堂・外（しばらく後）

喪の設(しつら)えがされた店。
その表を、大八車(だいはちぐるま)を引いて、通り過ぎる北斎の姿。

北斎「（店の方を見やり）……」

60　北斎の家（引越し先の長屋）・表

小綺麗な裏路地。

61　同・内

シン、とした室内。荷解きもされず雑然とした部屋に、ポツンと座る北斎。
目の前には、紙と筆。
北斎、波を題材に絵を描き始める。

62　北斎の工房兼自宅（7年後）

歳を重ねた北斎（壮年期）。ひたすら、絵にのめり込んでいる。

字幕「弐の章」

相変わらず、質素な身なり。袖は墨で黒くなっている。
下絵の積まれた工房の中を、せわしなく動き回る弟子たち。
すると――

北斎、ふいに立ち上がり、描いていた絵を鷲掴みにする。
驚き、振り返る弟子たち。
しかし、北斎は無言のまま、戸も閉めずに出かけていく。

弟子たち「……（ポカンと）」

63 江戸の町

夏の、賑やかな通りを行く北斎。

64 馬琴の家・書斎

夢中で原稿を書く滝沢馬琴（前の瑣吉）。背後の棚には、著書の数々が積まれている。
その目の前の文机に、唐突に放られる挿絵。馬琴、驚いて顔を上げると、北斎がぬっと立っている。

北斎「続きは書けたか？」
馬琴「……その前に言うことがあるだろう」

北斎　「……絵ができた」

馬琴。その物言いに呆れつつ、

馬琴　「おめえ、ひでえツラだな」

北斎　「……」

馬琴　「少しは休んだらどうなんだ？」

北斎　「おめえが言えた義理じゃねえだろ。日がな一日、机にばっかかじりついてよ」

馬琴。何を言っても無駄と原稿を渡し、筆を置く。

馬琴の原稿に目を落とす北斎。

その場で絵を描き始める。

馬琴　「ここで描くのか？」

北斎　「絵が見えたんだ。さっさと描かねば消えちまう」

馬琴　「だからって……」

北斎　「すまんが、ちょっと黙っててくれ」

馬琴　「……」

65　北斎の工房兼自宅（真夜中）

物音を立てぬよう帰ってくる北斎。
部屋の奥では、妻、コトが眠っている。
北斎。疲れ切った様子で、隣に敷かれた布団に崩れ落ちる。

66　同（翌朝）

蝉の声で、目を覚ます北斎。
枕元に置かれた、着替えの着物。
布団から起き上がると、コトが朝餉（あさげ）の準備をしている。
その様子を眺める北斎。

北斎「（穏やかな表情で）……」
コト「（気付き）お目覚めですか？」
北斎「ん。あぁ……（モゴモゴと返答）」

コト「すぐに支度しますね」
北斎「……」

67　馬琴の家・書斎

向かい合って作業する北斎と馬琴。
蝉時雨の中、二人が鎬を削り、筆を走らせる音が部屋に響く。
と、馬琴。北斎に絵を突き返して、

馬琴「これはダメだ。悪いが描き直してくれ」
北斎「(顔を上げ)？」
馬琴「絵が話を食っちまってる」
北斎「どういう意味だ？」
馬琴「絵がでしゃばってるってことだ」
北斎「……」
馬琴「俺が書いてないことを、おめえさんが勝手に描き足しちまってる」
北斎「そう見えたんだから仕方ねえ」

馬琴「(解せず) 見えたって、どこに見えたんだ」
北斎「(目を指し) ここだ。この奥だ」
馬琴。北斎の目を見つめる。
北斎「おめえの書いた話がここに浮かんだ」
馬琴「……」
呆れながらも、その言葉が嬉しくもある馬琴。
馬琴「だからって、おめえさんに勝手に描かれちゃ、話の辻褄(つじつま)が合わなくなるんだ」
北斎「だから、どうした? 俺は俺で、物語を描いている」
馬琴「……?」
北斎「読み手は挿絵で、想像を広げるんだ。チマチマしたもんなんて、描きたくもねえ」
馬琴「……」
北斎「俺は俺の好きに描くだけだ。遠慮する気なんざぁ、さらさらねえ」
馬琴「(言葉を失って) ……」

68 北斎の工房兼自宅

北斎の弟子たちに、食事の支度をするコト。
美味しそうに頬張る弟子たち。

コト　「（笑みを浮かべ）」
給仕を続ける。

×　　×　　×

縁側。
照りつける日差しを見上げるコト。ふと、お腹を触り、微笑む。

コト　「……」

69　屋形船

新たな戯作原稿を持ってきた版元（はんもと）・山崎屋。

山崎屋　「（やや興奮気味に）先生。この戯作は、ぜひ一度お読みください」
北斎。受け取るが、半信半疑で、

北斎　「……おめえさんが持ってくんのは、いつも変わりばえしねえもんばかりだ。……てんで、絵が浮かばねぇ」

それでも、山崎屋。原稿をめくる北斎に押し切るように、

山崎屋「柳亭種彦（りゅうていたねひこ）といいます。これなら、先生だってダメとは言わねえはずだ」

北斎「（ページを繰り）妖怪ものか」

山崎屋「（強く）時が経つのを忘れますよ」

読み始める北斎。

山崎屋「いつか必ず、当代きっての戯作者になる人だ。この山崎屋が約束します」

70　夜の山中（北斎のイメージ）

不気味な雰囲気。木々が生い茂り、梟（ふくろう）が鳴く中、ひとり座り込んでいる北斎。

（北斎による戯作挿絵のイメージ）

71　北斎の工房兼自宅

種彦の戯作を夢中になって読んでいる北斎。時折、筆を走らせるように、手が無意識に動いている。

コトがお茶を出してくれるが、気付かない。

コト「……」

コト、何か言いたげに立っているが、原稿から顔を上げない北斎に、諦めて踵を返すと。

北斎「何か言ったか？」

やっと北斎が、顔を向ける。

コト「……いえ」

うまく言い出せないコト。

コト「……夢中で読んでらっしゃるなぁ、と」

北斎「……あぁ」

コト「(微笑み) お茶を淹れましたから、一息ついてください」

北斎「ん……(茶を啜り、原稿を見つめ)……柳亭種彦、か」

72 屋敷・座敷 (日替わり)

通人たちが集まっての、百物語の会。

北斎、馬琴、山崎屋などが車座になっている。
蝋燭が灯る中、今しも、怪談がひとつ語り終えられたところ。
そこへ。暗い空間に光が差し込み、山崎屋の手代が狼狽して駆け込んでくる。

手代　「旦那様！」

山崎屋　「？」
手代、何事か山崎屋に耳打ちする。

山崎屋　「（動転して）！」
その表情に集まった面々も、耳をそばだてる。

山崎屋　「（見回し）……歌麿先生が捕えられたと」
一瞬にして、場が凍りつく。

馬琴　「何があったんだ」

山崎屋　「御禁令に背いた絵を描いた」

馬琴　「なにを今さら……。はなからそんな絵ばかりだろう。だいたい、お上の言いつけを守ってたら、まともな絵なんざ描けやしねえ」

山崎屋　「むろん見せしめだ。こういうなぁ目立つ方から潰していくんだ」

北斎　「……」

馬琴「出る杭は打たれる、ってことか。蔦屋の旦那も言ってたな」
その言葉に苛立ちを見せる北斎。
北斎「それで歌麿は？」
手代「許しが出るまで揚屋入りだそうで。手鎖されて五十日……」
一同「……」
馬琴「大人しく反省しろって話か」
北斎「（憤然と）人が喜ぶ絵を描くのが、そんなに悪ィことか？」
馬琴「お上からすりゃ、面白くねえのさ。黙って働けってこった。怒るな笑うな喜ぶな。知恵がつくから泣いてもくれるな」
北斎「……」
北斎。怒りを堪え、立ち上がる。
馬琴「おい。どこへ行く？」
北斎「……帰る」
馬琴「（訝って）こんな日まで仕事する気か？」
北斎「こんな日だからだ」
突っぱねるように言い放つ。

73　北斎の工房兼自宅（夕）

じっと、墨を擦る北斎。

74　同（真夜中）

自室へ帰ってくる北斎。
すると、コトが待っていて。

北斎　「起きていたのか？」

コト　「……えぇ」

また何か言いたげなコト。が、北斎の顔が曇っているのを見て取って、黙ってしまう。

北斎　「なんかあったか？」

コト　「いえ。……えぇ（と、頷く）」

北斎　「（不安になって）……なんだ？」

コト　「（口ごもりながら）……子ができました」

北斎　「？」
コト　「子を、授かりました」
　北斎。なんと言っていいか分からず、口ごもる。
北斎　「……」
　その表情どこか陰って見え、
コト　「嬉しくはございませんか？」
北斎　「……」
コト　「（も、戸惑って）……」
　俯く。
北斎　「すまねえ。ただ、こんな時代に生まれた子が、本当に幸せになれんのかって」
コト　「……」
　その表情に、微かな憤りが生まれ、
コト　「笑ってくださいませんか？」
北斎　「……」
コト　「そんな顔じゃ、幸せなどやってくるわけがないでしょう！　この子はお腹の中で、生まれてくるのを待ちわびているんです。私たちが喜んでやらなくてどうするんですか！」

北斎「……」

コトの物言いに面食らいながらも、そっと、コトのお腹に手を差し出す。

北斎「いいか？」

コト「（頷き）」

北斎の手を取ってお腹に当ててやる。

北斎。その温かさを感じて。

北斎「……」

笑みを見せる。

75 同・庭（時間経過）

絵を描きながら、生まれたばかりの娘（お栄）を、ぎこちなくあやす北斎。隣で、

コトも幸せそうに微笑んで――

北斎、お栄と戯れながらも、筆を走らせる。

76　北斎の工房兼自宅（23年後）

字幕「参の章」

江戸の外れの、荒れ地。ポツンと建つ、一軒家。

庭は一切手入れがされず、散らかり放題の部屋は、もう何ヶ月も掃除がされていないようだ。

その片隅にちょんと置かれているのは――コトの位牌。その周りだけが、かろうじて綺麗にされている。

布団の中から、ムクリと起き上がる老人――北斎（老年期）である。

77　同・外

のんびりとした足取りでやってくる、武家姿の戯作者、柳亭種彦。

絵の具の材料に使う植物を採って、帰ってきたばかりのお栄が出迎える。

種彦「お栄殿」
お栄「お、種彦。随分と早いね」
種彦「朝まで原稿、書いていてね。早く先生に読んでもらいたくてさ」
お栄「そりゃ、大変だ」
種彦「……あれからどうだい？　先生の様子は？」
お栄「（首を傾げ）……まぁ。どうだろうな。おっかぁが死んでからってもの、頑固親父がよけい固まっちまって、まるで地蔵みたいだ。朝から晩まで、絵ばかり描いていて……」
種彦「……そうか」
お栄が背負子（しょいこ）を下ろすのを手伝う種彦。
お栄「種彦が来れば、親父どのも気が紛れる。ゆっくり話していってくれ」

78　同・内

北斎が黙々と絵を描くところに、花を持って入ってくる種彦。後ろからお栄も続き、その手に持つ背負子を弟子の高井鴻山（たかいこうざん）が受け取る。

種彦　「（部屋に上がりながら）北斎先生。おはようございます」
北斎　「（振り向かず）おはよう」
北斎の横に、原稿を置く種彦。
種彦　「……すっかり涼しくなりましたね」
北斎　「ん」
種彦　「（持参の花を出し）これを」
北斎　「（見て）……喜ぶな」
種彦　「……」
北斎、また絵に没入している。その背中、どこか淋しそうで、
種彦　「……」

79　小普請組寄合所・内

広い板張りの部屋。黒光りする床板。
並び座る武士たち。
厳粛な空気が漂う部屋。その中に、種彦の姿もある。

支配頭、永井五右衛門の訓示が始まる。

五右衛門「昨今の世の混迷は目に余るばかりであるが、これすなわち市井の風紀の乱れに帰するものである。世を賑わす享楽的な読み物や浮世絵。中でも、合巻などという地本に女子供までもが手を出す様は、不届きの極みと言わざるを得ない。我々は武家の矜持をしかと持ち、世を乱す物事を厳しく律していかねばならぬ」

種彦「……」

無表情で聞いている。

80　江戸の町（秋）

庶民たちが、ささやかな日常を生きる姿。

その中を、北斎が行く。

81　種彦の屋敷・書斎

立派な屋敷。

その書斎で、向かい合って仕事をする北斎と種彦。

傍らには北斎と種彦の共作が並び、北斎はその一冊を読んでいる。

種彦の妻、勝子がお茶を置いて出ていくと、

種彦　「まったく、ひどい言い草だ。さも、庶民の読む本は悪とでも言うかのようだ。まるで、武家は生まれながらに格上で、庶民は低俗だと決めつけている」

五右衛門の訓示を批判する種彦。

北斎　「言わせたい奴には言わせておけ。イキり立っても仕方ねえ」

種彦　「……」

北斎　「おめえさんも、不自由なもんだな。種彦」

種彦　「……」

北斎　「俺は若え頃、地位も名誉も金もねえのが不自由だと思っていたが……おめえさんの方がよっぽど不自由だ。しゃっちょこばった武家でいながら、戯作を書いてんだから」

種彦　「……」

北斎　「変わんねえもんだな、世の中ってなぁ」

82 北斎の家兼自宅（夜）

ひとり布団で眠る北斎。
隣に、コトの位牌。

北斎「……」

83 道

歩く北斎。
行き交う人々。江戸の日常の風景。
そこにふいに風が立ち、町人たちの笠が飛ばされ、裾が翻（ひるがえ）る。

北斎「（見て）……」

思わず写生帖を構え、絵を描き始める。
夢中で筆を走らせる北斎。

×　×　×

躍動感ある、軽妙な絵が仕上がっていく。
(『北斎漫画』の一コマ)
北斎。我を忘れて没頭するが……
その線がふいに、微かにブレる。
北斎「(違和感を感じ)……?」

84 北斎の工房兼自宅

入ってくる北斎。
お栄。振り向いて、
お栄「どこほっつき歩いてたんだい? 西村屋、もう帰っちまったよ」
北斎「(朦朧と)」
土間に立ちすくむ。
お栄「絵が刷り上がったって持ってきてくれたのに」
北斎「……」
その顔、みるみる青ざめ、バタンと倒れる!

お栄　「（驚いて）親父どの！　親父どの！」
駆け寄るお栄、弟子たち。
北斎の視界……何事か叫ぶ弟子たち。が、北斎にはその声は聞こえない。

85　同（しばらく後）

床に伏せている北斎。お栄が薬を持ってくる。
北斎。半身を起こし湯呑みを受け取るが、手が震える。

北斎　「……」

86　同・外（日替わり）

見舞いにやってきた種彦。お栄の顔にけ疲れが滲む。

お栄　「卒中だ。命は助かったが、肝心な手に痺れが出ちまった」
種彦　「……」
お栄　「生きてるだけ御の字だと皆は言うが、あの親父にそんなこと言えるわけねえ」

種彦「……」
お栄「もう筆は持てなくなるかもしれん。まったく、参っちまうな」
種彦「先生は……」
お栄「奥で寝てるよ」
お栄。肩を落とし、
お栄「（ぼそり）おっかあがいればな……」

87 同・内

北斎「（二人の話を聞いている）……」
効かなくなった右手を見つめて。

88 同・内（日替わり）

病み上がりの体を立たせ、紙の前に立つ北斎。
どうにか絵を描こうとするが、手が満足に動かない。

無様に揺らぐ線。

北斎「……」

筆を置く。

89　同（日替わり）

家の外。朽ち果てた大木の周りを歩く北斎。

×　×　×

工房内では、お栄が版元（はんもと）、西村屋と話している。

西村屋「……今までがむしろ、元気すぎたくらいですよ。一時も休まず、働きっぱなしで。しかし、さすがの北斎先生だって限界ってもんがある」

お栄「……」

西村屋「淋しいが、潮時ってもんかねぇ」

お栄「……そりゃ、どういう意味だい?」

西村屋「お栄さん。あんたが引き継ぐ気はないかい?」

お栄「?　あたしゃ女だよ」

西村屋　「もちろん、工房を継ぐのはあんたにゃ無理としても、次ができるまで親父さんの代わりをやりゃいいじゃないか」

お栄　「（ムッとして）あんた、親父がもう描けないって言うのかい？」

西村屋　「……（無理だろうという顔）」

お栄　「見損なったよ、西村屋。あんた今まで親父の何を見てきたんだい！」

西村屋　「いや、そんなつもりは……」

お栄　「じゃあ、どういうつもりだ！　代わりなんているわきゃねえだろ！」

西村屋　「しかし……」

お栄　「うるせえ！　あんな絵ェ描けんのは、親父しかいねえんだ！」

西村屋　「……」

辺りのものを蹴散らすお栄。

お栄　「帰っとくれ！」

西村屋　「（唖然と）……」

お栄　「帰れ！」

驚いて、逃げ去る西村屋。

表から、その様子を見ていた北斎。考えこむように、

北斎　「……」

90　種彦の屋敷・中庭（しばらく後）

座敷で花を生ける勝子。
その間から続く中庭では、北斎と種彦が話している。

北斎　「おめえさんにも迷惑かけちまったな。まったく情けねえや」

種彦　「北斎先生のおかげで、今の私があるんです」

種彦「いえいえ」と首を振り、

北斎　「……」

ぼんやりと中庭を見る。
その目線を、やや動きが出てきた右手に移しながら、

北斎　「おめえさんの挿絵描くの、楽しみだったんだが……。面白くてな。絵を描いていると、こっちが若返っていくようだった」

種彦　「（笑む）」

北斎　「だけど、歳ってもんは嘘をつかねえな。七十（しちじゅう）は七十だとお栄にも怒られちまった」

種彦「（笑む）」

北斎「だけどな、種彦。何も悪いことばかりじゃねえ。病になったら、急にやりてえことを思いついた」

種彦「？」

北斎「しばらく旅に出る」

種彦「そのお身体で？」

北斎「あぁ……」

種彦「……」

北斎「こうなっちまった今だから見えるもんが、きっとあるはずだ」

種彦「（北斎の意を汲んで）……」

91　北斎の工房兼自宅

不自由な右手を庇いつつ、行李（こうり）を広げる北斎。わずかな着替えと写生帖を詰めていく。

その様子を半ば諦め顔で見ているお栄。

お栄　「どうせ止めても無駄だろうが……」

北斎　「（手を動かしながら）あぁ。無駄だ」

お栄　「……（笑い）見送りはしないよ」

北斎　「喋ってないで、仕事に戻れ」

お栄　「宿はどうすんだ?」

北斎　「そんなもん、行った先で探すんだ」

お栄　「なかったら?」

北斎　「その辺で転がるしかねえな」

お栄　「（嘆息し）これだからなぁ……」

と、コトの位牌を取りにいき、何事か話しかける。

行李を風呂敷に包み、立ち上がる北斎。

お栄。北斎にコトの位牌を渡す。

北斎　「……」

受け取り、何も言わずに出ていく。

92　旅路

行李を背負い、杖をつきながら北斎が歩いていく。

美しく広がる風景。

×　×　×

さらに、ひた歩き――

北斎。道端に咲く一輪の花に、足を止める。

背中の荷を下ろし、懐から写生帖を取り出す。が――

筆を構えたところで手を止める。

北斎「……」

まだ痺れの残る手。

北斎。写生帖を懐に戻し、その花をただじっと見つめる。

93　旅路（日替わり）

さらに歩いていく北斎。
その目は木々、鳥、虫、働く人々……。
あらゆるものを、一途に見つめていく。

94　浜辺への道

杖をつき歩く北斎。
ふいに眼前の道が開き、海に辿りつく。
遠くに見える小さな富士。波の音——

北斎　「……」

×　×　×

砂浜に座る北斎。傍にコトの位牌を置き、海を眺める。

95　峠道（早朝）

薄暗い道を歩いていく北斎。険しい道に息が荒れる。
朝日が昇り、徐々に辺りが明るくなってくる。
峠道の頂上。北斎の目が大きく開かれる。
ご来光を受け、紅く染まった富士が現れる——

北斎「（心奪われ）……」

96　北斎の工房兼自宅（少し後）

懸命に習作を描く北斎。手はまだ治りきってはいないが、以前より快方に向かっている。
感覚を呼び起こすように、何度も同じ線を引く北斎。
お栄と弟子たち、その姿を見て。

お栄「……」

97　種彦の屋敷・書斎

文机の上に置かれた、書きかけの原稿。
種彦。縁側に座り、庭を見つめて。

種彦「……」

98　北斎の工房兼自宅

質素な食事をしている北斎。
右手はほぼ、もとの動きを取り戻している。
そこへ入ってくるお栄。種彦の読本を手に、

お栄「(北斎に差し出し)『偐紫田舎源氏』――種彦の本だ」
北斎「(チラと見る)」
お栄「(やや心配そうに) 若えモンにえらい人気だ。刷りが追いつかねえくれえだって」
しかし、北斎はさらっと、

北斎　「いいじゃねえか」

お栄　お栄。その軽さを訝って、

北斎　「種彦は武家だぞ。あたしらとは違う」

お栄　「本を書くのに武家も町人もねえ」

　　　「武家だからこそ、睨まれたらただじゃすまねえって言ってんだ」

北斎　と。北斎。箸を止め、

　　　「(語気強く) なら、おめえ。種彦を止めにいってこい」

お栄　「……」

北斎　「できると思うか？　処罰を怖がって、俺が絵をやめると思うか？」

お栄　「――種彦と親父どのじゃ、身分が違う」

北斎　「本を書きてえ者が、たまたま武家に生まれたってだけだ」

お栄　「親父どのは、種彦が心配じゃないのか？」

北斎　「……」

　　　一瞬、黙り込む北斎。

北斎　「自分が書きてえものを、ただ吐き出し、それが人の心を打つ。冥利に尽きるじゃねえか」

お栄　「……」

北斎　「止められるもんじゃねえよ。おめえだって、そうじゃねえのか？」

99　同（日替わり）

絵を描く北斎。

100　同（日替わり）

激しい雨が工房を打ち付けている。その中、ベロ藍の絵の具を見つめる北斎。お栄、鴻山ら弟子たちも、その様子を見守っている。
絵の具の色合いを、細かく見極める北斎。

北斎　「……！」

唐突に唸りをあげると、ベロ藍を鷲掴みにし、雨の降る外へと飛び出していく！
雨音、祝福するが如（ごと）く、鳴り響き……

101　同（日替わり）

胡坐をかき、しばし白紙を見つめる北斎。
雑念を払うように、目を閉じる。

北斎「……」

やがて――
目を開くと、一気呵成に筆を走らせていく。
狂気をはらんだ眼差し。

×　×　×

『冨嶽三十六景　神奈川沖浪裏』が出来上がる。

102　彫師・摺師工房

その絵が彫師、摺師の手によって、次々と完成されていく。

103 西村屋・店頭

次々押し寄せる客。
我先にと『冨嶽三十六景』を買っていく。

104 家々

『冨嶽三十六景』を持つ手。
町人、武家、かかわらず、様々な人の手に取られ、家々に飾られていく。

105 種彦の屋敷・書斎

『冨嶽三十六景 神奈川沖浪裏』を手にする種彦。

種彦「……」

106　北斎の工房兼自宅

字幕「四の章」

ピンと張りつめた空気。
新しい、北斎の工房。飾り気のない、シンプルな空間。
お栄、鴻山、弟子らと共に、創作に集中する北斎（晩年期）。
新入りの少年弟子、喜三郎（きさぶろう）が方々の手伝いをして動き回る。

107　種彦の屋敷

冬を迎えた中庭。
書斎では、種彦が原稿を書いている。花を生ける勝子。立ち上がり、

勝子「（何か言いたそうに）……」
種彦「（気付いて）？」

顔を上げると、

勝子「いえ」

と、首を振り、

勝子「どうぞ。ご無理なさらずに」

部屋を出ていく。

種彦「……」

108　小普請組寄合所・内

冬景色の中庭。その脇の長い渡り廊下を、五右衛門と歩いてくる種彦。

五右衛門「高屋殿。実は、妙な噂を耳にしてな。そなたの家に、柳亭種彦という戯作者が居候していると」

種彦「……」

五右衛門「存知おるか」

種彦「（躊躇いつつ）……いえ」

五右衛門「それは何より」

種彦　「……」

五右衛門「下らぬ世迷い言を世に書き散らす不逞の輩と、そなたの様なわきまえた人物が知り合いのはずがない」

種彦　「……」

五右衛門「よろしいか？」

種彦　「……」

どうにか頷いて見せる種彦。

109　北斎の工房兼自宅

笑い声が響く工房。
故郷へと旅立つ鴻山のために、弟子たちが「雀踊り」を見せている。それに合いの手を入れながら、笑って眺める北斎、お栄、種彦。
しかし、種彦の表情には、時折、暗い影が見える。

北斎　「（気付いて見る）……」

×　　×　　×

鴻山　盛り上がる宴席。その輪から、鴻山、抜け出てきて。
「（北斎の前に座り）先生、本当にお世話になりました」
と、頭を下げる。
北斎　「（頷く）」
鴻山　「ここを出るのは……淋しいですが。どうぞ、お達者でいらしてください」
北斎　「鴻山もな」
鴻山　「（笑み）江戸の暮らしに慣れちまって、小布施（おぶせ）の田舎暮らしに戻れるか心配ですが」
お栄　「いつでも戻ってくりゃいいさ」
北斎　「（笑う）」
鴻山　「……よかったら先生も、遠いところですが、一度いらしてください。山しかないが、
飯と空気はここよりうまいです」
北斎。笑って、
北斎　「しかし、六十里も行くのは、この体ではな」
鴻山　「……」
北斎　「たまには便りでもよこしな」
鴻山　「（頷き）」

再び、宴の輪の中へと戻っていく。
北斎。浮かぬ顔の種彦が気になり、声をかけようとするが、その直前、種彦は立ち上がり、席を外す。
遅れて追う北斎。
宴席では、喜三郎の歌う信濃の唄が、朗々と始まる。

110 同・庭（夜）

庭。種彦と北斎。喜三郎の唄が聞こえてくる。

種彦「今日は冷えますね」
北斎「……」
種彦「……北斎先生」
北斎「？」
種彦「先生は、絵のために全てを捨てられますか？」
北斎「……」
種彦「お栄さんも、お弟子さんたちも、なにもかも。……すみません、こんな問いを。

北斎　無意味ですよね」
　その言葉の意味するところを、じっと考える北斎。
種彦　「いつかは……いつかは人に指図されねぇで生きていける世の中が来る」
北斎　「……」
種彦　「生きてるうちに、そんな世の中が見てぇ」
北斎　「私もです……」
　「俺は……俺にできることをやるだけだ。種彦……」
　地面に、指で波を描く北斎。
　種彦、無言で立ちつくす。

111　同（日替わり）

　朝一番に来て、掃除をする喜三郎。
　北斎、入ってきて、その様子を見つめる。
北斎　「……」

112　種彦の屋敷・外

寄合所へ出かける種彦。勝子に送り出されるが、ふと思いついたように振り返る。

種彦「……勝子」

勝子「……？」

種彦「……この冬が開けたら、旅に出てみるか」

勝子「……旅に？」

種彦「あぁ。たまにはゆっくりと」

勝子「……」

種彦「花でも見ながら」

勝子「ええ、ぜひ」

種彦「（笑み）行ってくる」

頭を下げる勝子。

113　北斎の工房兼自宅

一心に、描いている喜三郎。

見守る北斎。

北斎「……」

114　小普請組寄合所（暗闇に近い、閉め切った部屋）

対座する種彦と五右衛門。

五右衛門、種彦が著した新作の戯作を前に叱責する。

五右衛門「これはいったいどういうことだ」

種彦「……」

五右衛門「そなたの家の居候、追い出せと忠告しただろう！」

種彦「……居候とは……」

五右衛門「（制し）黙れ！　たまたま面倒を見てやっていた下賤無頼（げせんぶらい）の徒が、幕府の政（まつりごと）を茶化すような下らない物を書いていた。そやつから迷惑を受けたお主は、家から追い出した。それで万事解決じゃ。分かったな」

と、立ち上がる五右衛門。

種彦　「(呼び止め) お待ちください。……できません……私には」

五右衛門　「高屋彦四郎！　武士というものを、なんと心得る。高屋の家がどうなるか分かった上での、今の言葉か！　のう！」

種彦　「……」

五右衛門　「何を血迷ったことを！　高屋の家を滅ぼすつもりか？　妻子を路頭に迷わすつもりか！」

種彦。その言葉に、

種彦　「……」

拳を握りしめ、自己問答する。

五右衛門、本を床に叩きつけ、

五右衛門　「捨てよ！　下らぬ姿を！　下らぬ心根を！　話はこれまでだ」

と去ろうとするが、

種彦　「お待ちください」

種彦　五右衛門を呼び止め、向き直る。
「私はやめません。……書くことを、やめません」
種彦、顔を上げ、五右衛門を見返す。
種彦　「……私が柳亭種彦です。それを捨てることはできません」
軽蔑するように睨む五右衛門。
背を向けて去る。

115　北斎の工房兼自宅

絵に向かう喜三郎。
北斎　「(見て)……」

116　小普請組寄合所

五右衛門を筆頭とした武士たちに囲まれる種彦。
種彦　「……！」

117　北斎の工房兼自宅

喜三郎の描線を見る北斎。
そこへ、激しい足音が近づいてくる。

お栄「親父どの！」

血相を変え、やってくるお栄。

北斎「(振り返る)」

お栄「種彦が…… 種彦が……！」

北斎「……!!」

118　種彦の屋敷・門前

息を切らし、やってくる北斎、お栄。
固く閉ざされた門扉を懸命に打ち叩く！

119　同・部屋

顔に覆いを被せられた種彦の遺体が布団に寝かされ、頭の部分には首桶（くびおけ）が置かれている。

種彦の元に座る北斎、お栄。勝子もその隣に座している。

勝子　「主人は自ら、命を絶ちました」

北斎　「……」

勝子　「武家の名に恥じない、立派な最期だったと」

北斎　「――お勝殿」

立ち上がり、退席する勝子。その表情。

北斎　「……」

種彦の覆いを外す。

お栄　「！」

歯を食いしばり、嗚咽を漏らすお栄。

北斎　「……」

目を閉じる。

120 北斎の自宅兼工房（日替わり）

静寂。

弟子たちの姿はない。

喪失感に打ちひしがれた北斎。それでも——

筆を取る。

そこへ、肩を落とし、入ってくるお栄。

お栄「（驚いて）親父どの。こんな日にも絵を描くのか？」

北斎。紙に向かい、

北斎「こんな日だからだ」

121 同（時間経過）

薄明かりの中、紙の前に座り、静かに目を閉じる北斎。

目を開くと――

×　×　×

イメージ。種彦が殺される様が展開する。
侍たちに囲まれる種彦。
窮地の中、必死で抵抗するが、刀が種彦に突きつけられる。

×　×　×

まっすぐ前を見続けている北斎。

×　×　×

イメージ。
刀、種彦の首をめがけて振り下ろされる。

×　×　×

目を閉じる北斎。
恐ろしい絵が部屋に置かれている。
『生首図』
首を斬られた男の断末魔の叫び。男は口を開き、何かを伝えようとしている。

122　同（日替わり）

『生首図』の前に座る北斎。
その後ろに立つお栄は、慄然（りつぜん）として。

お栄「親父どの、この絵は……」
北斎「……」
お栄「こんな絵がお上（かみ）の目に触れたら、今度は親父どのが捕まっちまう……」
北斎「お栄」
お栄「……」
北斎「わしは、種彦がどんな男だったか、分かっておる」
お栄「……」
北斎「自害などする男ではない。口を封じられたんだ。言うべき言葉も言えねぇまま」
お栄「親父どの」
北斎「……」
お栄「江戸を出よう。お願いだ。たった一度でいい。私の頼みを聞いてくれ」

北斎　「……」

お栄　「……親父どの！」

と、床に手をつく。

北斎　「……」

『生首図』を見る。

123　険しい山道

荷を背負い、杖をつきながら、北斎とお栄が歩いていく。

北斎、ひたすら念仏を唱えている。

124　山道

ひた歩く、北斎とお栄。

鴻山の声　「先生！　北斎先生！」

駆けてくる鴻山。

二人。今にも倒れそうに、顔を歪めて……。

125　小布施・碧漪軒（アトリエ）（日替わり）

北斎、薄暗い部屋でうずくまるようにして、何かを描いている。
念仏を唱えながら、一心不乱に描いているのは……
魔除けの獅子図。
北斎の、狂気と哀愁に満ちたその表情。

126　同・外

お栄とともに、来る鴻山。

127　同・内

『生首図』を手にする鴻山。

向かいに座る北斎、お栄。

鴻山　「この絵は、私が預からせていただきます」

北斎　「……すまんな」

鴻山　「(首を振る)」

北斎　「(絵に目を向け) 何も変わらねぇんだな」

鴻山　「?」

北斎　「九十年近く生きてきて、同じものばかり見せられてきた……」

鴻山　「……」

長い間。やがて、

鴻山　「……変わりますよ」

ボソリと言う。

北斎　「……?」

鴻山　「きっと、いつかは……」

お栄　「……」

北斎　「……」

『生首図』にしばし目を落とし、ふと目を上げる北斎。

北斎「鴻山。今ひとつ、頼みてぇ」
鴻山「は？」
北斎「絵が、描きてぇんだ」
鴻山「……」
北斎「（思いを噛み締め）この目の中に、言葉が見えるんだ」
と、目を指す。
鴻山「言葉？」
北斎「あぁ。言葉だ。こいつを、ここに残してぇ」

128 小布施（おぶせ）・蔵（少し後）

大判の板の前、座禅を組む北斎。
目を閉じ、心を鎮めている。
北斎「……」
目を開けて立ち上がるや、絵の具を筆に含ませ、一気呵成（いっきかせい）に絵を描き始める。
老いの滲んだ体に力を漲らせ、食らいつくように筆を走らせる、北斎。

その目は、ここではないどこかを睨むようだ。
いつしか若き日の北斎も姿を現し、二人の北斎が重奏するように、筆を走らせる。
静寂の中、時に穏やかに、時に荒れ狂うように跳ねる筆。
鮮やかな藍色が、躍る――

× × ×

どことも知れぬ、空間。
その中央に――
怒涛図『男浪』『女浪』が置かれている。
そこに、北斎の声。

北斎の声

「己六才より物の形状を写の癖ありて
半百の比より数々画図を顕すといへども
七十年前画く所は実に取に足ものなし
七十三才にして
稍禽獣虫魚の骨格草木の出生を悟し得たり
故に八十才にしては益々進み
九十才にして猶其奥意を極め

一百歳にして正に神妙ならんか
百有十歳にしては一点一格にして
生るがごとくならん
願くは長寿の君子
予が言の妄ならざるを見たまふべし」
（『富嶽百景』跋文より）

完

脚本家・河原れんインタビュー

脚本家は映画の設計図を描く仕事

映画『HOKUSAI』の企画者でもあり脚本も担当した河原れん。
今回の映画に込めた思いや制作秘話を語っていただきました。

――河原さんは葛飾北斎の何をいちばん描きたかったんですか?

北斎の生き様を描きたいと思っていました。生来の天才がブレイクしたのではなく、荒削りの人間が苦労して壁を乗り越え、北斎だけが得られる高みに到達したという話にしたいと考えました。

――台本は何稿まであったのでしょう?

準備稿が13と、その後に大きな直しのない稿が2つありました。撮影に入るまでの約2年の間に、15稿まで書きましたね。

――初稿はどんな台本だったんですか?

最初は江戸に大火が起きたり、当時の日本橋を再現するシーンも書いていました。そしたら、「これは20億円ぐらいかかる脚本だよね」ってプロデューサーから却下されて。それから予算面だけでなく、物語の構成にも苦労しました。北斎の脂がいちばんのっていたのは70歳以降かもしれないけれど、老年期だけだと若い観客層の支持を得にくい。青年期も老年期も描くのが物語としてはベストだけど、90年の人生をどう描けばいいか、頭を抱えましたね。世界一有名な日本人でありながら、北斎を題材にした映画が多くはない理由が分かりました。

——具体的には、それからどうしたんですか？

基本に立ち返って、自分だったら北斎の何を見たいのか?を考えたんです。間違いなく、北斎の人生そのものを見たいし、やはり波なくして北斎は語れない。それで、波に至るまでに何があったのか?という点を重層的につなげるという構成が浮かんだんです。

——次にしたことは？

年表と照らし合わせながら、誰と誰がどんな風に出会っているのか?を探っていきました。そしたら、歴史的には重要視されていないけれど、版元(はんもと)の蔦屋重三郎が営む耕書堂から、北斎が挿絵を描いた本が出版されているのに気付いて。しかも重三郎が亡くなった直後に、北斎が人気絵師に化けたので、そこに何かドラマがあったのでは?と思ったんです。ここからは私の創作ですけど、青年期と老年期にそれぞれの山場を作らなければいけないと思っていたので、青年期は重三郎との出会いをそれにしました。

——青年期・老年期にはそれぞれ特徴的なキャラクターが出てきます。

そうですね。滝沢馬琴や喜多川歌麿、東洲斎写楽も北斎と同時代を生きた人物です。それで青年期は、北斎が彼らと創作に関して火花を散らすシーンを書き、次に老年期では、幕府の弾圧で処罰された柳亭種彦を象徴的に登場させ、この映画のテーマを投影する人物にしたんです。

——種彦はあまり有名な人ではないですね。

私も当時は知らなかったんですけど、調べたらものすごいベストセラー作家だった。なのに、なぜ処罰されたのか？　しかも、種彦が処罰された年に北斎が『生首図』を描いている。あんな不気味な絵を描いたのには何か理由があるはずだ！　そう思ったときに、種彦との関係を老年期のクライマックスにできるのではないか？って閃いたんです。でも、実は、橋本一監督は種彦を登場させることに最初は否定的でした。

——どうしてですか？

知名度がないし、泣き落としみたいなクライマックスは避けたいと思われたんでしょうね。でも私は、種彦は自分が見つけた想像的事実だと思っているので、落としたくなかった。種彦がいないと、北斎が自然にある境地に達して成功した話になって、青年期の重三郎の存在も希薄になってしまう。それに重三郎と種彦は「幕府から処罰を受けた後に死亡した」という共通点もあった。さらには喜多川歌麿も処罰されている。これらの点を線でつなぐことができれば、説得力のあるストーリーが作れると思いました。

——何稿でその構成に？

10稿ぐらいでやっと気付いたという感じですね。8稿ぐらいまではボロボロでした。それこそ私は、完成度の低いホン（台本）しか書けなくて、撮影を一度延期させているんです。崖っぷちに立つような思いで書き続けましたが、8稿のときには想像力も働かず、出がらしみたいになっていました。それでも、どうにか書き上げたものを締切日に出したら、中山賢一プロデューサーから「もう降りた方がいいよ」って言われてしまって。

——8稿に足りなかったのは？

いろんな人がただオールスター大集合みたいに出てくるような内容で、何も心に響かないものだったんです。

——「降りた方がいいよ」って言われて、素直に引き下がったわけではないですよね。

8稿を出した日に仕事でフィンランドに行かなければ

ばいけなかったので、成田空港で中山さんに謝り続けていたんですけど、そのときに「君が帰ってくるころには新しい脚本家を用意しているから」って言われて。でも、こっちが悪いし、自分の能力がないだけだから、どうしようもない。なので、「分かりました」って言いました。ただ、その後に「もう一度チャンスをください」ってお願いしたんです。

——向こうで書き直したんですね。

機内で食事もせずにプロットを作ったんですけど、北極に近いマイナス30度のロバニエミという街に着いたら、パソコンが凍って動かなくなったんです。あのときはもうダメだ〜って思ったけれど、中山さんに言い切ったからには何とかしようと思って、手で書き上げました。

——何日間で仕上げたんですか？

6日間ぐらいで書いたんですけど、東京に帰ってきてそれをパソコンで打ち直したらちょうど2時間の尺で、中山さんにも「これならいけるんじゃない」と言ってもらえて。北斎だから北極星に近いところで書いたのがよかったのかもしれないし、手で書いたので頭の中のイメージを、より直接的にストーリーやセリフにのせられたんだと思います。

——圧倒的に変わったのは？

例えば青年期の北斎が海に入るシーンも、8稿までは重三郎が北斎を海に連れていって開眼させるものだったんです。

——それを北斎が自分で発見するように設定し直したんですね。

そうです。でも、それって難しくて。海に入った北斎が突然ハッと開眼したら嘘っぽいし、自分自身で気付くためにはそれに足るだけの苦悩がないといけない。それで写楽の宴席のシーンなどを足したんです。

——写楽にナメられるところですね。

自分より能力のある人に違いを見せつけられたら、それこそ生きていけない。そこは「もう降りた方がいいよ」って言われたときの私と少しだけリンクしていました（笑）。誰もが天才で生まれて天才として散っていくわけではないので、主人公の苦悩はきちんと描きたかった。だから、北斎をひたすら苦しめたんです。ただ、お金や身分ではなく、絵で苦しむ姿を映像で伝えるのはそう簡単ではない。絵の上手い、下手は見た人の主観でしかないですからね。それこそ、北斎は美人画も上手いんですよ。均整がとれていて、歌麿の美人画よりも美しい。それに、重三郎が歌麿や写楽を育てたのは事実なので、北斎の個性も見抜いて投資したはず。その証拠に北斎が〝可候〟の名で描いた美人画の代表作『風流無くてなゝくせ』は重三郎の耕書堂で刷られているんです。だからその絵をわざわざ出して、「勝ち負けで絵を描いているのか？」と重三郎が北斎の心を見透かし、プライドをへし折るシーンを足したんです。

――北斎の苦悩の背景を足したんですね。

それが以前の稿にはないから、突然出てきた人が都合よく何かをしゃべって、傷つけて消えていくみたいな感じだったんです。やはり、背景を深彫りしないと、人物が薄っぺらくなってしまう。種彦にしても、彼がなぜああいう思想や感情になったのかが分かるように、小普請組の寄合所で支配頭の永井五右衛門から厳しく警告されるシーンをプラスして。重三郎も「吉原の実家の遊郭は弟に継がせた」という設定を後から足して、チャキチャキの江戸っ子というキャラを強調したんです。

――そこまで苦労されたことも踏まえて、河原さんの今の気持ちを教えてください。

衣裳を担当された大御所の宮本まさ江さんが「ホンが面白かったから、私がエキストラさんの着付けもしているのよ」と言ってくださったり、「このホンだから、出たいと思った」という永山瑛太さんや「今回のようにホンが面白ければやりますよ」という阿部寛さんの言葉を聞いたときは、目頭がちょっと潤んでしまいました。落語家の立川志の輔さんは「心が震えるぐらい感動した」との感想をくださって。あの8稿のときの苦しみがあっただけに、このストーリーをみなさんが評価してくださったときは本当に報われたような気がしました。

——やってよかったですか？

もちろんです。確実に成長しましたから。脚本家は多くのプロフェッショナルが携わる映画の設計図を描く仕事なので、中途半端なことは絶対にやってはいけない。その職人としての腹積もりも、『HOKUSAI』をやる前と明らかに変わりました。

——一生懸命やらなければいけないと？

台本は一生懸命やれば書けるものではありません。一生懸命やるのは当たり前だし、パソコンが壊れても手で書いた私のように、メンタルも含めて最悪な事態になっても乗り越えられる自分を作っておかなければいけない。追い込まれても、希望を見い出しながら一個一個問題点をクリアして書き続けるしかない。そのときの自分にできるすべてを注ぎ込んで、必死にやるしかないんです。

2007年、『瞬』で小説家デビュー。同作は2010年に映画化（監督：磯村一路）。映画『余命』脚本（監督：生野慈朗）、小説『聖なる怪物たち』、ノンフィクション小説『ナインデイズ―岩手県災害対策本部の闘い』など、様々なジャンルにわたり執筆。本作にはお栄役で出演もしている。

冨嶽三十六景　神奈川沖浪裏

Thirty-six Views of Mt. Fuji / The Great Wave off Kanagawa

上町祭屋台天井絵　怒涛図 男浪（北斎館蔵）

Kanmachi Festival Cart Ceiling Panels / Angry Waves : Masculine Waves
Property of the Hokusai-kan Museum

上町祭屋台天井絵　怒涛図 女浪（北斎館蔵）

Kanmachi Festival Cart Ceiling Panels / Angry Waves : Feminine Waves
Property of the Hokusai-kan Museum

江島春望

Spring at Enoshima

Screenplay

CONTENTS

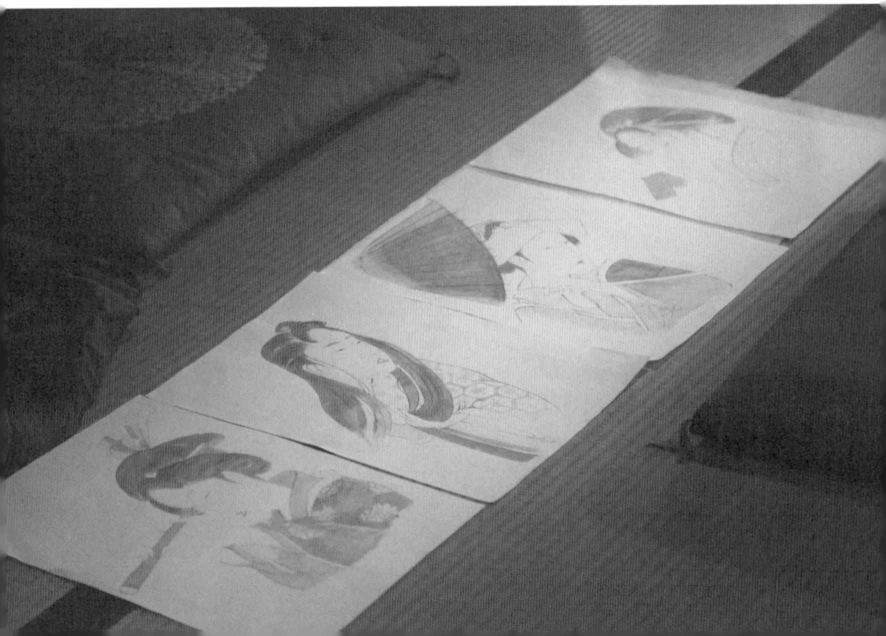

Illustrated novels and hand-drawn paintings, Katsushika Hokusai Period

In the Kansei era of reform, the Shogunate government began regulating publishers strictly, but regulation of literature remained relatively lax. Hokusai capitalized on the opportunity and produced over 1,400 illustrations for 190 books over a decade. This is when he began collaborating with Takizawa Bakin and Ryutei Tanehiko.

"Awa No Naruto"
Property of the National Institute of Japanese Literature

First collaboration with Ryutei Tanehiko

Rinpa School/ Tawaraya Sori, Hokusai Tokimasa Period

After leaving the Katsukawa School, Hokusai joined the Rinpa School and earned the name of Tawaraya Sori II. He established his own

"Seven Foibles of Young Women: The Telescope"
Property of Hagi Uragami Museum

age 75-90 1834-1849 | **age 71-74** 1830-1833 | **age 53-70** 1812-1829

Later Life, Hand-drawn Paintings Period

Later in life, Hokusai devoted himself wholly to hand-drawn paintings. His style became more realistic and profound, and his motifs also took a dramatic turn from genre paintings to historical Japanese and Chinese themes, religious art, and paintings of natural creatures. Hokusai died in 1849 in Asakusa at the age of 90.

"Feminine Waves"
Property of the Hokusai-kan Museum

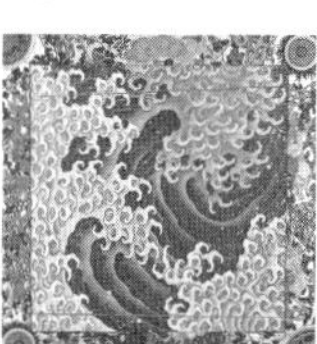

"Masculine Waves"
Property of the Hokusai-kan Museum

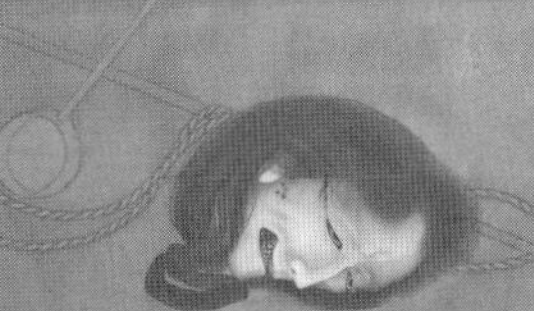

"Severed Head"
Painted at the time of Tanehiko's death

Colored Prints Period

Hokusai produced many works depicting birds and flowers as well as colored prints during this period. Leveraging the trend of reverence toward Mount Fuji, he published the immensely popular

"Thirty-six Views of Mt. Fuji: The Great Wave off Kanagawa"

The birth of the "Wave"!

Chronology of Hokusai's work

Katsukawa Shunro Period

Became a disciple of painter Katsukawa Shunsho. Received the name Katsukawa Shunro in his first year by demonstrating exceptional promise and talent. Presented a variety of work from illustrations of actors, comic books, paintings of children, toys, samurai, famous sites, sumo wrestlers to religious motifs.

"Actor Iwai Hanshirō IV as Kashiku"
property of The Sumida Hokusai Museum

Sori style with freedom and boldness that set himself apart from the Katsukawa and Rinpa School artists. He challenged himself with woodblock prints, illustrations for comic tanka poems, paintings of slender, beautiful women, hand-drawn paintings and color prints. He left the Rinpa School in 1798 and changed his name to Hokusai Tokimasa.

"Spring at Enoshima"
An early glimpse of the "Wave"?

age 0-18	age 19-34	age 35-44	age 45-52
1760-1777	1778-1793	1794-1803	1804-1811

Art Manuals (Sketchbooks) Period

The birth of "Hokusai Manga", illustrated sketchbooks meant as instructive manuals for his disciples throughout Japan. It was also meant as a collection of artistic design manuals. During this period, Hokusai delighted the public with performances like painting two tiny sparrows on a grain of rice right after a 60-foot dharma on a huge sheet of paper.

"Sketches by Hokusai, Vol.3"
property of The Sumida Hokusai Museum

series "Thirty-six Views of Mount Fuji", introducing landscapes into the ukiyo-e genre for the first time. Other examples of his artistic breadth include paintings of phantoms in "100 Ghost Stories" and paintings of Japanese board games.

"Peonies and Butterfly"

1A. On the road

Under a blazing sun, Hokusai (about 10 years old), bathed in sweat, draws intently on the ground with a stick. A group of neighborhood bullies surround him and stomp all over his drawings.

Hokusai glares and lunges at them, but is quickly overpowered and beaten.

He scowls as he struggles repeatedly to get up.

1B. A room in a brothel

In a candle-lit room, Hokusai (now an adolescent) is painting a nude courtesan lying opposite him. His face glistens with sweat as his brush moves feverishly. He seems more aroused by his own imagination than the woman posing provocatively in front of him.

1C. Hokusai's house and studio

A torrential downpour pummels the eaves of Hokusai's dilapidated studio. Hokusai (now an old man) bursts out of his studio. His hands, holding indigo blue paint, are raised to the sky. Hokusai glows in a cascade of blue as rain and paint fuse together.

The vivid image overlaps with the title "HOKUSAI"

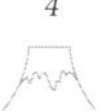

2. Hokusai's tenement house / Exterior

A worn-looking alleyway covered in mud and filth.

3. Hokusai's tenement house / Interior

In a dimly lit room, Hokusai's drawings are strewn carelessly about: drawings in the Katsukawa-style, Kano-style, Chinese style, studies of western paintings, sketches…

In a corner of the room, a young Hokusai is painting peonies with youthful, obsessive strokes.

CAPTION: Chapter I

4. In an Edo bookshop: Tsutaya Koshodo / Exterior

A *noren* (shop curtain) bearing the crest of Mt. Fuji flutters in the breeze.

Suddenly, government officials barge in, shoving customers roughly aside.

GOVERNMENT OFFICIAL
This is a raid!

Chaos consumes the bookshop. The intruding officials enter with their shoes on, treading over the books and woodblock prints. Customers are kicked out and salesclerks are knocked down.

5. Tsutaya Bookshop / Interior

GOVERNMENT OFFICIAL

Tsutaya Juzaburo, owner of Tsutaya Bookshop!

The man who confronts the overbearing official is casual in his demeanor. He is Tsutaya Juzaburo, owner of the bookshop.

Juzaburo's wife Toyo and the employee Sakichi (later Bakin) look on worriedly.

JUZABURO

…

GOVERNMENT OFFICIAL

You are charged with causing social unrest and corrupting public morals. We will thereby confiscate half your property.

Government officials begin tossing merchandise into a bonfire on the street. In the commotion, the shop's Mt. Fuji *noren* falls and also catches fire.

JUZABURO

…!

Juzaburo glares at the official. The official returns his glare, but then draws back slightly, intimidated.

The shop is in chaos. While printing blocks and paintings are burned, one after the other, Juzaburo's fury also rages silently.

JUZABURO

…(Trying to control himself)

6. Hokusai's house / Interior

The walls of the tenement are paper thin. Hokusai is surrounded by women's voices and household noises, but he is oblivious to the din as he mixes his paint.

7. Tsutaya Bookshop / Exterior to interior

The shop has been ravaged by the officials. Toyo, his wife, resolutely picks up a broom and begins sweeping. Clerks follow her lead.

Sakichi picks up a drawing by Kitagawa Utamaro from the ashes. Juzaburo takes it and dusts off the soot with his sleeve.

JUZABURO
Even covered in soot, it's provocative. No one can paint a woman like Utamaro.

SAKICHI
You're right.

JUZABURO
I guess I should be grateful.

SAKICHI
(Looking up) ?

JUZABURO
They say a protruding nail gets hammered down.
This just proves that, as a publisher, I'm head and shoulders above the rest.

Juzaburo smiles slightly.

TOYO
…

SAKICHI
…

JUZABURO
(Looking around the shop) I've cultivated the greatest painters and authors. This is quite amusing. It's like a shower of blessings.

SAKICHI
…

JUZABURO
Now all of Edo will be watching to see what I do next. It's the ideal moment to plant new seeds.

8. Hokusai's house

Hokusai is finishing up a brilliant painting of peonies.

9. Yoshiwara (Red-light district) / Omon Street (Night)

Juzaburo strolls down the busy street.

10. Minoya / From the counter to the reception room

A brothel in the Yoshiwara District (Juzaburo's family home)

The owner Genjiro, Juzaburo's brother-in-law, approaches Juzaburo.

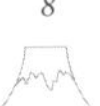

GENJIRO
Brother!

JUZABURO
(Smiling) You look busy.

GENJIRO
(Also smiling) I'm managing.

JUZABURO
You're finally getting the hang of the business.
It's as if I'm looking at my old man.

GENJIRO
Cut it out. I'm nowhere near that. In fact, I was just having trouble dealing with a brawl between guests.

JUZABURO
Every night is a festival around here.

Loud noises are heard as a fight breaks out in the back.

GENJIRO
(Tsk-ing) These country bumpkin samurais.

JUZABURO
Samurais, merchants – they're all men. Once they set foot in here, their leashes come off.

× × ×

The two men go upstairs and walk down a hallway. Juzaburo is holding a sake bottle. *Shamisen* music and women's laughter can be heard through the paper screen doors.

Juzaburo stops at the last room and opens the screen door.

JUZABURO
…

Kitagawa Utamaro sits with a sheet of paper in front of him. He is painting with a look of rapture on his face. Nearby, a half-naked courtesan with a dreamy expression lounges in a supine pose.

Juzaburo enters loudly and puts the sake bottle down on the tatami mat.

UTAMARO
(Looks at him)…

Utamaro acknowledges Juzaburo with a flick of his chin. Several completed paintings lie on the table.

JUZABURO
(Looking satisfied)

He takes the paintings and makes to leave.

UTAMARO
I hear there's a courtesan in Nishikiya named Asayuki.

JUZABURO
(Looks back)

UTAMARO
I hear she has beautiful eyes.

JUZABURO
(Nods) I'll summon the girl from Kyoto if that's what you want.

UTAMARO
…

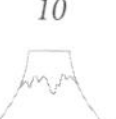

Juzaburo exits.

11. Nishikiya (Another brothel) / Interior

Asayuki holds a pipe and eyes Juzaburo suspiciously.

ASAYUKI
No, thank you.

JUZABURO
Why not? It's not a bad proposition.

ASAYUKI
I don't like painters, that's all.

JUZABURO
…(With imploring eyes)

ASAYUKI
They have no manners. Why, one of them had me standing all night long.

JUZABURO
Sounds like a passionate painter to me.

ASAYUKI
(Laughs through her nose) You must be kidding. More like a monkey with no manners. He had the nerve to climb right on top of me, claiming he couldn't get the lines right.

JUZABURO
(Laughing) It must have been an exquisite painting.

ASAYUKI
Of course, it was. I was the model. But I'll never do

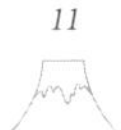

that again.

Asayuki blows out smoke.

ASAYUKI
I'll never pose for a monkey with no manners.

12. Tsutaya Bookshop / Interior (The following day)

Sakichi finally gets it and nods emphatically.

SAKICHI
I know who that is! It's Shunro. Katsukawa Shunro.

JUZABURO
"Katsukawa"?

SAKICHI
We've commissioned a few ourselves. (Laughing) "Monkey with no manners", huh? The courtesan has a way with words.

He goes to retrieve a few of Hokusai's paintings drawn under the pseudonym "Shunro."

Juzaburo takes them.

JUZABURO
(Staring at the pictures)···

SAKICHI
He has talent but he's a pain in the ass. He only paints what he wants to paint. And once he gets started, he won't quit until he's satisfied···

JUZABURO
(Intrigued···)

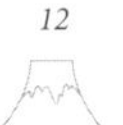

SAKICHI
I have no idea what he's doing now.

JUZABURO
He's not with the Katsukawa school?

SAKICHI
He was excommunicated long ago.

JUZABURO
Excommunicated?

13. On temple grounds

Hokusai is trying to sell his paintings.

SAKICHI
(Voiceover)
When it comes to painting, he sees no reason. He experimented with the aristocratic Yamato-e style paintings while in the Katsukawa school. He even tried out the Kano style. In the end, he punched out a senior disciple.

JUZABURO
(Voiceover)
Punched out…? But why?

SAKICHI
(Voiceover)
Who knows?

Hokusai's demeanor is boorish. Passersby don't give him a second glance. He stares off into the distance with a weary, resigned look on his face…

14. Hokusai's house / Exterior

Hokusai returns home. He hears the kid next door being scolded by his mother.

He senses a presence as he opens the door.

HOKUSAI
…?

15. Hokusai's house / Interior

Hokusai enters, suspicious.

Someone has entered uninvited, and is looking at his paintings.

The man turns. It's Juzaburo.

HOKUSAI
Why, you're…

JUZABURO
…

HOKUSAI
You're from the bookshop.

JUZABURO
I wanted to take a look at your paintings. You took so long, I finally just let myself in.

HOKUSAI
What do you want?

JUZABURO
Just checking to make sure you were alive.

HOKUSAI
?

JUZABURO
That's what Sakichi said.

HOKUSAI
...

JUZABURO
So, are you surviving?

HOKUSAI
None of your business.

JUZABURO
...

HOKUSAI
Yeah, I sell a painting or two to keep myself going.

JUZABURO
Your paintings?

HOKUSAI
(Expression momentarily darkens) Yeah.

JUZABURO
Make any money?

HOKUSAI
…Hmph.

Juzaburo carelessly puts down a painting he was looking at.

JUZABURO
Why don't you come paint for me?

HOKUSAI
(His expression stiffens)

JUZABURO
I'll sponsor you. Make you famous.

HOKUSAI
...

JUZABURO
What's wrong?

HOKUSAI
No thanks.

JUZABURO
(Surprised)?

HOKUSAI
Sorry, but I'm not cut out to take orders.

JUZABURO
(Thinks for a while) I see.

HOKUSAI
...?

JUZABURO
I heard you punched out a senior disciple.

HOKUSAI
From Sakichi again?

JUZABURO
(Nodding) That's right. Why'd you do it?

HOKUSAI
He drew on my painting.

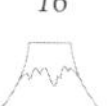

JUZABURO
…

HOKUSAI
And ruined it.

Juzaburo smiles slightly.

JUZABURO
I see. Sorry to bother you, then.

Juzaburo heads out the door.

HOKUSAI
(Watches him leave)…

16. On temple grounds (Another day)

Hokusai lays out his paintings at the same spot, but everyone just walks by.

HOKUSAI
…

17. Hokusai's house

Hokusai returns home.

When he opens the door, he sees a package bearing the Tsutaya family crest.

HOKUSAI
…

He opens the package. There's money inside.

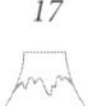

18. Tsutaya Bookshop / Interior

Hokusai comes to the bookshop, looking angry.

Sakichi is working on his novel while keeping shop. He looks up.

SAKICHI
…

He looks at Hokusai as if to say, "So you came after all."

SAKICHI
It's been a while.

HOKUSAI
…

SAKICHI
(Smiling) Looking for Master Juzaburo?

HOKUSAI
(Nods)

SAKICHI
He's in Yoshiwara.

19. Minoya / Exterior (Night)

Hokusai enters.

20. Minoya / Hallway

Hokusai is led down the hallway by a male servant.

21. Minoya / Reception room

Hokusai opens the sliding door loudly.

He sees Utamaro painting a portrait of Asayuki.

Hokusai is shocked.

UTAMARO
(Also shocked)…

Asayuki glares at Hokusai coldly.

ASAYUKI
…

JUZABURO
(Sarcastically) Well, well, well. Look who we have here.

UTAMARO
You know him?

JUZABURO
Just a painter I picked up by chance.

ASAYUKI
(Speaking over Juzaburo) A monkey.

Utamaro makes the connection.

UTAMARO
So you're the infamous Katsukawa Shunro.

JUZABURO
He's no longer associated with the Katsukawa school, though.

HOKUSAI
…

JUZABURO
Well, don't just stand there. Why don't you take a seat? Master Utamaro is going to paint the most beautiful flower in Yoshiwara.

Asayuki looks away, annoyed.

Hokusai stands there, glumly, refusing to sit.

HOKUSAI
…

UTAMARO
I don't care whether you sit or stand, but since you're here, how about a drink?

Raises a sake bottle to Hokusai.

HOKUSAI
I don't drink.

Hokusai glares, feeling out of place.

Utamaro laughs.

UTAMARO
Good for you. Tsutaya, he doesn't even drink. He'll make you loads of money.

JUZABURO
(Suppresses a smile)⋯

HOKUSAI
…

UTAMARO

Just sit down. There's good fish. Have some.

HOKUSAI

I don't like fancy food.

Utamaro laughs loudly.

UTAMARO

(To Juzaburo) Did you hear that? Is he really a painter?

JUZABURO

It seems so.

UTAMARO

He's more like an ascetic monk. No wonder his women don't come alive on the page.

HOKUSAI

?

UTAMARO

The women you paint have no sex appeal.

HOKUSAI

…(Feeling slighted)

UTAMARO

Right, Tsutaya?

JUZABURO

…

Asayuki glances sideways at Hokusai.

UTAMARO

I'm not saying you're not talented. But…what you're

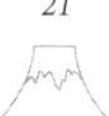

good at is producing a replica of what you see in front of you.

Utamaro points at the fish head on the platter.

UTAMARO
It's just veneer. It's not alive.

HOKUSAI
...

His blood pressure is visibly rising.

JUZABURO
(Watching him)

Hokusai can't tolerate this abuse any longer and turns to leave.

JUZABURO
Hey.

Juzaburo stops Hokusai.

JUZABURO
Running away?

HOKUSAI
...

JUZABURO
You're not the only one.

HOKUSAI
?

JUZABURO
Painters are a dime a dozen.

HOKUSAI
…

UTAMARO
…

Upon hearing Juzaburo's comment, Utamaro says

UTAMARO
Sorry, but can you shut that?

HOKUSAI
?

Hokusai hesitates, but sees fire in Utamaro's eyes. He shuts the sliding door and sits down. Juzaburo stares at the two painters.

Utamaro crumples the painting he was working on.

UTAMARO
(To Asayuki) Now for Mistress Asayuki…

ASAYUKI
(Looking up coyly at Utamaro) ?

Utamaro picks up his brush.

UTAMARO
Sit with your back facing me.

ASAYUKI
…(Like this?)

Utamaro gazes at her, caresses the nape of her neck, then… boldly rips open the collar of her kimono.

ASAYUKI
(Without time to protest)!

She strikes a languid pose with the collar of her kimono wide open.

UTAMARO
Hold this mirror, will you?

Asayuki looks demurely into the mirror. Utamaro's eyes take on an otherworldly glow. He pauses.

After a brief moment, Utamaro readies his brush and begins painting with fluid strokes. His lines flow like water. He barely looks at Asayuki as he paints.

HOKUSAI
…

22. Tsutaya Bookshop / Interior (The next day)

Sakichi is working on his novel. He senses a presence and looks up, only to find Hokusai standing there.

SAKICHI
(Looking up) Oh, it's Shun…

HOKUSAI
…

Hokusai stares down brazenly at Sakichi.

HOKUSAI
Does Utamaro always live there?

SAKICHI
Yes. He eats, sleeps and paints in that room at the brothel.

HOKUSAI
…

SAKICHI
We take care of all of it. It's quite a sum.

HOKUSAI
Why do you pay it?

SAKICHI
(Laughing bitterly) Master Juzaburo made him live there. He surrounded him with women to make him paint.

HOKUSAI
(Shocked)

SAKICHI
Our shop is going broke, thanks to him. The government already took away most of our money. (Mutters under his breath) And Master Juzaburo doesn't even read my novels.

HOKUSAI
?

Sakichi's manuscript has many editorial marks.

SAKICHI
So, what are you going to do? Paint for him?

HOKUSAI
(Doesn't answer) Well, here. (He hands him the package of money)

SAKICHI
?

HOKUSAI
Return it to him, will you? He left it at my house, but I can't take it.

SAKICHI
The master left it?

HOKUSAI
Yeah.

SAKICHI
…So you're not going to paint for him?

HOKUSAI
…

23. Hokusai's house

Hokusai is painting women's faces as if possessed.

24. Tsutaya Bookshop / Reception room

Hokusai lays out four paintings of women ("Seven Habits of Grace and Disgrace" series) with a nervous look on his face. Juzaburo (his health is beginning to fail) sits opposite him and examines the paintings. Sakichi looks on, shocked by Hokusai's artistry.

JUZABURO
…

Juzaburo looks disappointed.

JUZABURO
What is this?

HOKUSAI
What do you mean?

SAKICHI
(Looks questioningly at Juzaburo)

HOKUSAI
Look carefully. It's better than Utamaro's!

JUZABURO
Is it a contest to you?

HOKUSAI
...

JUZABURO
Why do you paint?

HOKUSAI
What do you mean?

JUZABURO
Exactly what I said. Why do you paint?

HOKUSAI
How should I know?

JUZABURO
...

HOKUSAI
I come from a poor family. I was sent away as an apprentice when I was three years old because they couldn't afford to feed me. I did what I had to do to survive.

JUZABURO
Then why did you become a painter?

HOKUSAI

Because I thought I could claw my way to the top. Social class doesn't matter to a painter. As long as you're good, you can··· (make it)

JUZABURO

(Spits out) Then, stop.

HOKUSAI

?

JUZABURO

If that's the stupid reason holding you back, then stop painting altogether.

HOKUSAI

What did you say?

JUZABURO

...

Juzaburo throws down some coins and leaves.

Hokusai is dumbfounded.

HOKUSAI

(Angrily) What the hell?

SAKICHI

...

HOKUSAI

That bastard!

Hokusai is furious. He leaves the paintings and the money.

25. Minoya / Reception room (Night)

Sake bottles and art supplies are strewn about the floor.

Utamaro is in bed with Asayuki.

Even while enraptured by her, he's observing and tracing her body.

26. Hokusai's house (Another day, day into night)

Hokusai is painting. As usual, loud noises emanate from next door. His room is a mess, littered with attempted sketches.

HOKUSAI
(Stops painting)…

He puts down his brush.

He stares at the paper in front of him.

27. Tsutaya Bookshop / Interior

Juzaburo is sick, and his eyes are slightly unfocused. His wife, Toyo, looks worriedly at his profile.

His brother-in-law, Genjiro, bursts into the room, overwhelmed with excitement.

GENJIRO
Brother!

JUZABURO
?

× × ×

He reveals a painting wrapped in cloth.

Juzaburo examines the painting. His face fills with surprise.

JUZABURO
Who painted these?

Genjiro smiles. This is exactly the reaction he expected.

GENJIRO
A customer of mine. He's still young, but he already knows how to have a good time.

JUZABURO
...

GENJIRO
He just paints for fun, but he's got loads of talent. I knew you'd see it.

JUZABURO
(Nods)

GENJIRO
He only paints *kabuki* actors. He watches *kabuki* and paints the actors for fun.

JUZABURO
...

GENJIRO
It doesn't look like a simple pastime to me.

JUZABURO
(Captivated by the paintings) Can I meet him?

GENJIRO
Of course. I heard he has more.

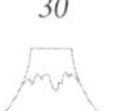

JUZABURO
(Excitedly) Then I'll buy them. All of them!

28. Hokusai's house / Exterior

Hokusai throws well water onto himself.

His hands won't stop sweating. He continues to rub his hands together.

HOKUSAI
(Pitifully)…

Hokusai wails.

29. Minoya / Juzaburo's room (Night)

Genjiro brings Toshusai Sharaku into the room. He still has a boyish look about him, but he wears a stylish kimono with casual ease.

Sharaku bows while Juzaburo greets him emphatically.

JUZABURO
I'm Tsutaya Juzaburo, owner of Tsutaya Bookshop.

SHARAKU
(Smiling) I've heard much about you.

JUZABURO
Please come in.

30. Hokusai's house

Hokusai is half-naked, finishing up a portrait of a woman.

31. Minoya / Juzaburo's room

Sharaku spreads out some paintings in front of Juzaburo, who looks on, eyes sparkling. Sharaku picks up a paintbrush and begins drawing effortlessly in front of Juzaburo's eyes.

32. Hokusai's house

After a monumental struggle, Hokusai finishes the painting.

33. Tsutaya Bookshop / Printing factory (Another day)

The printing factory is next to the bookshop.

Juzaburo's face is sallow, but he wills himself to oversee every detail of Sharaku's paintings as they are printed.

JUZABURO
Something's missing···

PRINTER
Missing···?

JUZABURO
I want the images to be etched into people's minds.

The printer is perplexed. Juzaburo has an epiphany.

JUZABURO
Mica.

PRINTER
Huh?

JUZABURO
Print them with mica!

PRINTER
That's unreasonable··· It'll eat away all our profits!

JUZABURO
(Smiling invincibly)

Sakichi comes calling.

SAKICHI
Master!

JUZABURO
?

34. Tsutaya Bookshop / Printing factory hallway

Hokusai waits in the reception room. Juzaburo observes from the hallway. Hokusai carries a wrapping cloth holding paintings. Juzaburo notices Hokusai's worried expression.

JUZABURO
(To Sakichi) Tell him to go home.

SAKICHI
What?

JUZABURO
I don't want his paintings.

SAKICHI
But···

JUZABURO
(Shakes his head)

He returns to the printing factory.

35. Tsutaya Bookshop / Interior to exterior

Hokusai takes his paintings, shoulders drooping.

SAKICHI
(Watching him leave)…

36. Hokusai's house (Another day)

Hokusai's eyes are unfocused. He continues to paint, undaunted, but he has run out of paint.

HOKUSAI
…

37. On temple grounds

Hokusai is selling his paintings again…without success.

38. On the road

Hokusai walks down a busy street and sees a crowd forming around Tsutaya Bookshop.

HOKUSAI
?

As he approaches…

39. Tsutaya Bookshop / Exterior

Sharaku is featured prominently.

HOKUSAI
(Shocked)

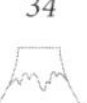

He is drawn inside.

40. Tsutaya Bookshop / Interior

Paintings of *kabuki* actors are on display, making a huge impact. Hokusai stares at each one, as if in a trance.

SAKICHI
(Sees Hokusai, but…)

He can't bring himself to call out to him. Juzaburo's voice is heard, talking to fellow art collectors.

Hokusai turns on his heels, but Juzaburo notices Sakichi looking at Hokusai.

JUZABURO
(To Hokusai) Hey.

Hokusai stops.

JUZABURO
Why don't you come and greet me? Since you've come all this way.

Hokusai turns around timidly. Sharaku's works are on display all around the shop. Juzaburo is in high spirits. Hokusai starts to say something, but seeing Juzaburo staring at him, swallows his words.

JUZABURO
His name is Toshusai Sharaku. It was love at first sight.

HOKUSAI
…

41. Minoya / Reception room

A party is underway to celebrate the debut of Sharaku's works. A fine feast is spread out before them. Courtesans brighten up the room.

Juzaburo walks around the room pouring sake, introducing Sharaku to top clients.

JUZABURO
This is Master Sharaku. No one can replicate his paintings. A true genius.

Hokusai sits alone in the back with a sullen look on his face.

A waitress comes to pour him some sake, but…

HOKUSAI
No thanks.

He turns her down brusquely.

CLIENT 1
(As Juzaburo pours sake into his cup) I can't believe the artist is so young. It's quite remarkable.

SHARAKU
(Smiles)

CLIENT 2
(To Juzaburo) You're quite an art dealer.

JUZABURO
No, no. This is all Genjiro's doing. He's the one who discovered Master Sharaku.

CLIENT 2
But you're the one who made his spectacular debut

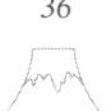

possible. Like fireworks.

HOKUSAI

…

Is listening, but barely able to tolerate it. Then, Utamaro makes a bold entrance into the room.

UTAMARO

Well, well. Everyone is here.

All the guests bow their heads simultaneously. Sharaku bows a moment later. Hokusai remains immobile.

UTAMARO

…

He sits at the head of the table, without even a glance at Hokusai. Sharaku quickly stands and pours Utamaro some sake, as Utamaro looks on.

UTAMARO

(To Sharaku) Nice work.

SHARAKU

?

UTAMARO

I'm talking about your paintings.

SHARAKU

(Bows)

UTAMARO

I was shocked. I never knew such paintings existed.

Shamisen begin to play as more courtesans enter the room. Asayuki enters last.

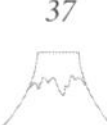

ASAYUKI
…

She glances at Juzaburo and sits next to Sharaku.

ASAYUKI
(To Sharaku) Congratulations.

She bows low and exchanges looks with Sharaku as Utamaro watches.

UTAMARO
…

Sakichi observes this scene play out from afar.

SAKICHI
…

Utamaro pours Sharaku some sake.

UTAMARO
I have one question. Do you actually see the *kabuki* actors like that?

SHARAKU
Like what?

Utamaro strikes an exaggerated pose like the *kabuki* actor in "Oniji" (Kabuki Actor Otani Oniji III as the Yakko Edobei) as if to provoke Sharaku.

SHARAKU
(Smiling) I wish I could take out my eyes and show you.

UTAMARO
(Laughs)

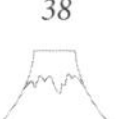

SHARAKU
(Smiling back) It would be boring to simply reproduce what I see in front of me.

He drinks from his sake cup. Asayuki flawlessly pours sake for Sharaku.

UTAMARO
It's more interesting to exaggerate?

SHARAKU
Oh, no. I'm just a mirror reflecting the actors' souls.

UTAMARO
...

Utamaro glances coolly at Sharaku and drains his sake cup. He turns down Asayuki's offer to pour and refills his cup himself.

Music from the *shamisen* and drums grow louder and the courtesans begin dancing. Hokusai is totally isolated.

HOKUSAI
...

Hokusai hangs his head, feeling out of place. Suddenly, his sake cup is filled to the brim. He looks up in surprise. Juzaburo is looking down at him.

HOKUSAI
I told you I don't drink.

JUZABURO
I know.

HOKUSAI
...

JUZABURO
I wanted you to raise your head.

HOKUSAI
How annoying.

Hokusai glares at Juzaburo.

JUZABURO
...

HOKUSAI
You call that a painting? Is that what you were looking for?

JUZABURO
(With confidence) Yes.

HOKUSAI
You must be kidding! He's not what I'd call a painter! Look at their faces and hands. They're not even in proportion! They all look like clowns!

JUZABURO
Master Sharaku is not a painter like you.

HOKUSAI
...?

JUZABURO
He's not affiliated with any school. He has no master.

HOKUSAI
Then how can he paint?

JUZABURO
(Glances at Sharaku)

SHARAKU

(Smiles unassumingly) I just paint for fun.

HOKUSAI

?!

UTAMARO

...

SHARAKU

Without much forethought, I was holding a brush and painting to amuse myself.

HOKUSAI

(Not getting it) Is this a joke?

SHARAKU

? (Puzzled)

HOKUSAI

Paint for fun? Impossible!

Hokusai is furious. He makes to get up. Sakichi comes quickly to his side and stops him.

SHARAKU

(Even more puzzled) I just paint what my heart tells me to.

Hokusai turns to Juzaburo, glaring.

JUZABURO

...

Juzaburo stares at Hokusai. Hokusai sits back down, speechless. He drops his gaze and sees a fish head on the platter.

HOKUSAI
…

42. Hokusai's house (Another day)

Sakichi has come over with a light snack for Hokusai, but the room is empty. Uncompleted paintings and broken pallets are scattered all over the room.

SAKICHI
…

43. On the road (Another day)

Hokusai wanders along the road with just a few personal items on his back.

44. On the road (Night)

Hokusai is camping out in the dark, an open wood fire burns. His eyes are open wide, staring at the flame. He tries to throw his case of paintbrushes into the fire, but can't bring himself to do it.

45. A country road (Another day)

Hokusai drifts down a country road.

46. At the gates of a temple

It's raining. Hokusai seeks shelter under the eaves. He's famished but has nothing to eat.

47. Tsutaya Bookshop / Hallway

Juzaburo looks up at the rain from the veranda. His profile looks worn. Toyo approaches.

TOYO
What are you doing out in the cold?

JUZABURO
Hm.

TOYO
I've been calling you. The doctor is here.

JUZABURO
Hm…

Juzaburo continues to stare at the rain.

48. On a road lined with dried, dead trees

Hokusai walks on, aimlessly, listlessly, an empty shell of his former self.

49. A grassy field (Evening)

Hokusai is so hungry he resorts to eating weeds. Repulsed, he gags and spits them out.

50. Minoya / Juzaburo's room

Juzaburo drinks alone, in a daze. Spread out on the floor is a world map.

51. A grassy field (After some time)

Hokusai is asleep. He is drained of energy and spirit.

A little later, he awakens to the sound of waves in the distance.

52. The ocean

Hokusai is drawn to the sound of the waves. He stops. It's the ocean.

HOKUSAI
(Unable to take his eyes off the water)…

He walks over to the surf.

The surf flows in and out.

Mt. Fuji rises majestically beyond the horizon.

Overcome with emotion, Hokusai takes out his sketchbook.

HOKUSAI
…

Hokusai tries frantically to capture the image. His frustration and irritation are overpowered by his fascination of the eternal ebb and flow of the waves.

He closes his eyes and listens to the waves. He is drawn to the water. The waves lap at his feet. He feels the crests of the waves on his skin. He goes deeper and immerses himself in the ocean. The sound of the waves, the smell of brine…

He tries to heighten his senses and absorb it all.

HOKUSAI
…

53. On the road in Edo

Hokusai returns to Edo.

54. Tsutaya Bookshop / Bedroom

Juzaburo is lying down, ill. Sakichi enters.

SAKICHI
Master…

JUZABURO
…?

× × ×

Toyo helps Juzaburo change into a kimono bearing his family crest.

55. Tsutaya Bookshop (The bookshop is closed) / Interior

Hokusai waits alone. There are no customers in the shop. Juzaburo struggles but manages to walk. He enters and sits opposite Hokusai. Toyo and Sakichi watch from afar. Juzaburo sees Hokusai's sunburned face.

JUZABURO
Looks like your journey did you some good.

HOKUSAI
(Looks at Juzaburo)…

But he has no words to say.

JUZABURO
I got tired of waiting for you. (Laughs bitterly) It's going

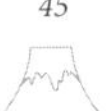

around in Edo. I don't have much longer.

He extends his hand.

HOKUSAI
...

Hokusai opens his wrapping cloth and hands Juzaburo some paintings.

JUZABURO
...

They're paintings of waves. Juzaburo is speechless. This is not what he expected.

HOKUSAI
I just painted what I felt like painting.

Juzaburo is drawn to the images.

HOKUSAI
If you don't want them, just say so.

JUZABURO
(Hokusai's confidence surprises him)···

Juzaburo glances at Hokusai.

JUZABURO
Waves, eh? ···I like it. Quite unexpected.

HOKUSAI
...

JUZABURO
These waves. Nothing like I've seen before, yet it is the epitome of a wave.

HOKUSAI
…

Juzaburo looks at the painting again.

JUZABURO
This is good.

HOKUSAI
…

JUZABURO
I want you to paint one for me.

HOKUSAI
(Looks at Juzaburo in surprise)

JUZABURO
…

56. Minoya / Hallway (Another day, night)

Courtesans and customers are bustling about.

57. Minoya / Juzaburo's room

Hokusai and Juzaburo look at a freshly printed "Spring at Enoshima." Juzaburo gazes with satisfaction at the print depicting Mt. Fuji on the horizon.

JUZABURO
I knew you had it in you.

HOKUSAI
…

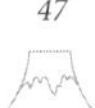

JUZABURO

Something only you could paint. Just like Mt. Fuji. There's no other quite like it. That's the unique beauty of it.

HOKUSAI

...

Hokusai finally breathes a sigh of relief.

Juzaburo pats him on the back.

JUZABURO

"Hokusai." The name suits you.

The signature under the print "Spring at Enoshima" reads "Hokusai Sori."

HOKUSAI

I borrowed the characters "Hokusai" from the North Star. It's the only star that stays put and never moves.

Juzaburo smiles at Hokusai's words. It's the first heartfelt smile Hokusai has seen from him.

Juzaburo tosses him a world map.

HOKUSAI

?

JUZABURO

Open it up.

Hokusai opens the map.

HOKUSAI

(Looking)···

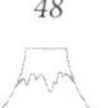

JUZABURO
In the scheme of things, (pointing) Edo is smaller than a grain of rice. Funny, eh?

HOKUSAI
...

JUZABURO
Whenever I look at this map, I get pleasantly drunk. I forget about everything and travel the world.

HOKUSAI
What lies beyond the ocean?

JUZABURO
Good food, good drink and good women. Paintings, too. Like you've never seen before. I'll open up a shop there.

Suddenly, a bright fire burns in Juzaburo's eyes.

JUZABURO
I'll discover new artists in a foreign land and sell their paintings. And show the world that my instincts are dead on.

HOKUSAI
...

Juzaburo empties his sake cup.

JUZABURO
I can't waste my time here. There's too much to do.

Juzaburo stands.

HOKUSAI
...?

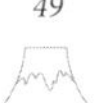

JUZABURO
I'll bring some sake. I feel like drinking today.

Juzaburo leaves the room, teetering. On the back of his kimono is his family crest: Mt. Fuji.

HOKUSAI
…

58. Juzaburo's funeral.

A long line forms outside. Tsutaya's associates all wear traditional coats bearing the Mt. Fuji crest. Toyo holds the memorial tablet. Sakichi and Genjiro follow.

59. Tsutaya Bookshop / Exterior (A short while later)

The shop is set up for mourning.

Hokusai passes by, pulling a large cart.

HOKUSAI
(Glancing at the bookshop)…

60. Hokusai's house (A new tenement that Hokusai has moved to) / Exterior

The alley is well-maintained.

61. Hokusai's house / Interior

Hokusai sits alone in a silent house full of unopened bundles from the move. In front of him are a brush and a sheet of paper.

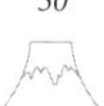

He begins to paint waves.

62. Hokusai's house and studio (7 years later)

Hokusai is older now. He is engrossed in painting.

CAPTION: Chapter II

Hokusai is dressed simply as ever, his sleeves blackened with ink. His disciples move busily about the studio. Rough sketches are piled high. Then…

Hokusai stands suddenly and clutches a painting he is working on. His disciples turn to look, shocked.

Hokusai walks out without a word, not even shutting the door behind him.

DISCIPLES
… (Puzzled)

63. On the road in Edo

Hokusai walks down a busy street. It is summer.

64. Bakin's house / Office

Takizawa Bakin (formerly Sakichi) is engrossed in writing a novel. His books are stacked up on the shelf behind him.

A handful of illustrations are dropped roughly onto his desk.

Bakin looks up in surprise. Hokusai is standing there.

HOKUSAI
How's the writing going?

BAKIN
Don't you have something to say first?

HOKUSAI
My illustrations are done.

Bakin is appalled by Hokusai's rudeness.

BAKIN
You look awful.

HOKUSAI
…

BAKIN
Why don't you get some rest?

HOKUSAI
I could say the same to you. You're scribbling at your desk all day, every day.

Bakin knows talking to Hokusai is useless, so he hands him his manuscript and puts down his brush. Hokusai looks at the manuscript. He picks up a brush and starts painting on the spot.

BAKIN
You're going to paint right here?

HOKUSAI
I had a vision. I have to capture it before it disappears.

BAKIN
But still…

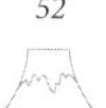

HOKUSAI
Sorry, but shut up for a moment.

BAKIN
…

65. Hokusai's house and studio (Middle of the night)

Hokusai returns home, trying not to make noise.

His wife, Koto, is sleeping in the back of the room.

A tired Hokusai takes off his kimono and crumbles onto the futon bed beside Koto.

66. Hokusai's house and studio (The next morning)

Hokusai awakens to the sound of cicadas and finds a new kimono set out beside his pillow. When he rises, he sees Koto preparing breakfast. He gazes at her.

HOKUSAI
(With a gentle expression on his face)…

KOTO
(Notices Hokusai watching) You're up.

HOKUSAI
(Mumbling in reply)…Yeah…

KOTO
Breakfast will be ready soon.

HOKUSAI
…

67. Bakin's house / Office

Bakin and Hokusai work across from each other.

Amid the humming of cicadas, the sound of brushes running furiously across paper echoes throughout the room.

Bakin hands a painting back to Hokusai.

BAKIN
This one's no good. Do it over.

HOKUSAI
(Looking up)?

BAKIN
The painting overpowers the story.

HOKUSAI
What do you mean?

BAKIN
Your painting is too bold.

HOKUSAI
…

BAKIN
Your painting is telling a story I haven't even written.

HOKUSAI
But that's what I see.

BAKIN
(Not getting it) Where did you see it?

HOKUSAI
(Pointing to his eyes) Here. Way back here.

Bakin stares at Hokusai's eyes.

HOKUSAI
Your story made me see it, here.

BAKIN
…

Bakin is flabbergasted, but flattered at the same time.

BAKIN
But if you just paint whatever you want, my story won't make any sense.

HOKUSAI
So what? I'm writing my own story.

BAKIN
…?

HOKUSAI
The illustrations will spark the readers' imaginations. I refuse to paint something small and timid.

BAKIN
…

HOKUSAI
I paint as I please. I don't hold back for anyone.

BAKIN
(At a loss for words)…

68. Hokusai's house and studio

Koto prepares a meal for Hokusai's disciples.

The disciples stuff their mouths, enjoying the food.

KOTO
(Smiling)⋯

She continues to wait on them.

× × ×

In the veranda, Koto looks up at the bright sun. She touches her stomach and smiles.

KOTO
⋯

69. On a houseboat

A publisher, Yamazakiya, brings a new light novel to Hokusai.

YAMAZAKIYA
(Excitedly) Master, you must read this light novel.

Hokusai takes it, warily.

HOKUSAI
The others you've brought me were boring. They don't conjure a single image.

The publisher insists while Hokusai flips through the pages⋯

YAMAZAKIYA
His name is Ryutei Tanehiko. I know you'll love this one.

HOKUSAI
(Flipping through the pages) A ghost story?

YAMAZAKIYA
(Emphatically) You'll lose track of time.

Hokusai begins to read the light novel.

YAMAZAKIYA
He will be the greatest writer of our time. I guarantee it.

70. In the mountains at night (In Hokusai's mind)

The atmosphere is unearthly. Hokusai sits alone in a thicket of trees. An owl hoots.

(An image of one of Hokusai's illustrations)

71. Hokusai's house and studio

Hokusai is engrossed in Tanehiko's light novel. At times, his hand moves as if holding an invisible brush. Koto serves him tea, but he doesn't even notice.

KOTO
…

Koto stands there, wanting to say something, but Hokusai doesn't look up from the manuscript. Koto gives up and turns around. Then…

HOKUSAI
Did you say something?

Hokusai finally looks up.

KOTO
No.

She has a hard time telling him.

KOTO
You're so engrossed in the novel.

HOKUSAI
Yeah…

KOTO
(Smiling) I made some tea. Why don't you take a break?

HOKUSAI
Hm…(he takes a sip of tea and stares at the manuscript) Ryutei Tanehiko, huh?

72. In a grand villa / Reception room (another day)

In a candle-lit room, members of the literary society have gathered to listen to ghost stories. Hokusai, Bakin and some publishers are sitting in a circle. One ghost story is reaching its climax. A shaft of light cuts through the dark space.

Yamazakiya's salesclerk stumbles in, flustered.

SALESCLERK
Master!

YAMAZAKIYA
?

The salesclerk whispers something to Yamazakiya.

YAMAZAKIYA
(Shocked)!

Everyone in the room listens intently.

YAMAZAKIYA
(Looking around the room) Master Utamaro has been arrested!

The room grows still.

BAKIN
What happened?

YAMAZAKIYA
He drew a painting that was banned.

BAKIN
This is old news··· He's always pushing the boundaries. If we all lived according to government codes, we'd never create anything of value.

YAMAZAKIYA
He's being scapegoated. They will crush anyone who is too flagrant.

HOKUSAI
···

BAKIN
A protruding nail gets hammered down. That's what Master Tsutaya used to say.

Hokusai is irritated by the comment.

HOKUSAI
So where is Utamaro now?

SALESCLERK
In a cell. He's being cuffed for 50 days.

EVERYONE IN THE GROUP
...

BAKIN
"Be quiet and reflect on your sins."

HOKUSAI
(Indignantly) Is it such a crime to paint what the people enjoy?

BAKIN
It's a slap in the government's face. They want us to shut up and work. Don't laugh or get mad or even cry. Emotions make for unruly commoners, don't they?

HOKUSAI
...

Hokusai stands, trying to control his anger.

BAKIN
Hey, where are you going?

HOKUSAI
To the studio.

BAKIN
(Skeptically) You're going to work on a day like today?

HOKUSAI
(He spits out roughly) That's exactly why I'm going to work.

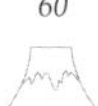

73. Hokusai's house and studio (Evening)

He rubs the ink stick in silence.

74. Hokusai's house and studio (Middle of the night)

Hokusai returns home. Koto is waiting.

HOKUSAI
You're still up?

KOTO
Yes···

Koto wants to say something, but Hokusai's brow is furrowed, and she clams up.

HOKUSAI
Is something wrong?

KOTO
No··· Well, yes. (She nods)

HOKUSAI
(Getting worried) What is it?

KOTO
(Mumbling) I'm with child.

HOKUSAI
?

KOTO
I'm pregnant.

Hokusai hesitates, not knowing what to say.

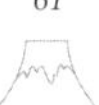

HOKUSAI
...

His expression is dark.

KOTO
Aren't you pleased?

HOKUSAI
...

KOTO
(Also at a loss)…

Koto looks down.

HOKUSAI
I'm sorry. But I wonder if a child born into this world can ever be happy.

KOTO
...

Her expression becomes angry.

KOTO
Please smile.

HOKUSAI
...

KOTO
You'll drive away happiness looking like that! This child inside me is just waiting to be born. We must welcome this child with joy!

HOKUSAI
...

Hokusai is shocked by Koto's vehemence. He quietly reaches over to touch her stomach.

HOKUSAI
Can I touch it?

KOTO
(Nods)

She takes Hokusai's hand and places it on her stomach.

Hokusai feels its warmth.

HOKUSAI
...

He smiles.

75. Hokusai's house and studio / Garden (After some time)

Hokusai awkwardly lulls his newborn daughter Oei while painting at the same time. Koto smiles happily nearby. He plays with Oei while moving his brush.

76. Hokusai's house and studio (23 years later)

CAPTION: Chapter III

A house stands alone on a barren plot outside Edo.

The garden is overgrown, the room is a mess.

It hasn't been cleaned for months.

A memorial tablet for Koto sits in one corner.

Only the area around the tablet is clean.

An old man rises from his futon bed. It's Hokusai (grown even older).

77. Hokusai's house and studio / Exterior

Ryutei Tanehiko, a light novelist, strides casually towards the house. He is dressed as a samurai. Oei has just returned with plants which will be used for pigments. She greets Tanehiko.

TANEHIKO
Miss Oei.

OEI
Tanehiko, you're early.

TANEHIKO
I was up all night writing. I couldn't wait for Master Hokusai to read it.

OEI
You must be tired.

TANEHIKO
How has he been?

OEI
(Shrugging) I don't know. Since Mom died, the stubborn old man has grown even more stubborn. He's like a stone statue. All he does is paint, day and night ...

TANEHIKO

I see…

He helps Oei with her load.

OEI

You're a nice diversion for him. Please stay awhile and talk.

78. Hokusai's house and studio / Interior

Hokusai is painting in silence. Tanehiko enters carrying flowers, followed by Oei. A disciple, Takai Kozan, takes her things.

TANEHIKO

(Entering the room) Good morning, Master Hokusai.

HOKUSAI

(Without even turning around) 'Morning.

Tanehiko lays a manuscript at Hokusai's side.

TANEHIKO

It's grown quite chilly.

HOKUSAI

Hm.

TANEHIKO

(offering the flowers) I brought these.

HOKUSAI

(Glancing at them) Koto will be pleased.

TANEHIKO

…

Hokusai goes back to his painting. He is engrossed, but also looks a bit wistful.

TANEHIKO
...

79. Meeting place of the Samurai Union / Interior

The floorboards of the large room are shiny and black.

Samurai are seated in a row. There is a dignified air in the room. Tanehiko is among them.

The leader, Nagai Goemon, begins with a proclamation.

GOEMON
The world today is full of confusion and chaos. This is due to the corruption of public morals which is encouraged by hedonistic literature and illustrations. What's more, these unethical "picture books" are accessible to women and even children. This is unforgivable. As samurai, we are bound by duty to uphold moral dignity and control these disturbing trends.

TANEHIKO
...

Tanehiko listens, expressionless.

80. A town in Edo (Autumn)

Townspeople are engaging in everyday activities. Hokusai walks among them.

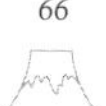

81. Tanehiko's villa / Office

In the office of his grand villa, Tanehiko and Hokusai work facing each other. Nearby are collaborative works of Hokusai and Tanehiko. Hokusai is reading one of them.

Tanehiko's wife Katsuko brings tea, then leaves.

TANEHIKO
This is ridiculous. They make it sound as if these picture books are the root of all evil. As if samurai are born superior and commoners are crude.

Tanehiko criticizes Goemon's proclamation.

HOKUSAI
Let them say what they want. There's no point getting angry over it.

TANEHIKO
...

HOKUSAI
You don't have much freedom, do you, Tanehiko?

TANEHIKO
...

HOKUSAI
When I was young, I thought having no position, title or money deprived me of freedom, but now I realize you have much less freedom than I do. You're a grand samurai writing light novels.

TANEHIKO
...

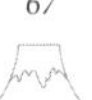

HOKUSAI

The world never changes, does it?

82. Hokusai's house and studio (Night)

Hokusai sleeps alone in his futon bed.

Next to him is Koto's memorial tablet.

HOKUSAI

…

83. On the road

Hokusai walks along the road, passing people along the way.

In the backdrop is daily life in Edo.

Suddenly the wind blows, toppling townspeople's bamboo hats and rippling their hemlines.

HOKUSAI

(Observing)…

Inspired, he grabs his sketchbook and starts painting. His brush moves excitedly.

× × ×

He puts the finishing touches on a witty scene full of lively movement.

(A scene from "Hokusai Manga")

Hokusai is lost in the artwork but…

His brushstroke suddenly wavers ever so slightly.

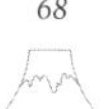

HOKUSAI

(Feeling something is amiss)…?

84. Hokusai's house and studio

Hokusai enters. Oei turns around.

OEI

Where were you, gallivanting around? The publisher Nishimuraya already left.

HOKUSAI

(In a daze)

Hokusai stands on the earthen floor.

OEI

He brought over some finished prints.

HOKUSAI

…

His face grows pale and he collapses.

OEI

(Shocked) Father! Father!

Oei and Hokusai's disciples run over to him.

Through Hokusai's eyes, disciples can be seen yelling to him, but he cannot hear what they are saying.

85. Hokusai's house and studio (A while later)

Hokusai is sleeping. Oei brings him his medicine.

Hokusai gets up halfway and takes the tea cup, but his hand

shakes.

HOKUSAI
…

86. Hokusai's house and studio / Exterior (Another day)

Tanehiko has come to pay him a visit. Oei looks exhausted.

OEI
He's had a stroke. He survived it, but his drawing hand is paralyzed.

TANEHIKO
…

OEI
Everyone says he should consider himself lucky to be alive, but I can't possibly tell him that.

TANEHIKO
…

OEI
He may never take up a brush again. I can't stand the thought of it.

TANEHIKO
Where is he?

OEI
In the back room, sleeping.

Oei's shoulders droop.

OEI
(Mumbles) If only Mom were here…

87. Hokusai's house and studio / Interior

HOKUSAI
(Listening to their conversation)…

He stares at his lame hand.

88. Hokusai's house and studio / Interior (Another day)

While still weak, Hokusai wills himself to get up and stand in front of a blank sheet of paper.

He tries to paint but his hand doesn't cooperate. His brush stroke is shaky.

HOKUSAI
…

He puts down his brush.

89. Hokusai's house and studio (Another day)

Hokusai walks around a great rotting tree outside his house.

× × ×

Inside the studio, Oei is in discussions with the publisher Nishimuraya.

NISHIMURAYA
It's a wonder this didn't happen sooner. He never rested and worked from morning to night. But even Master Hokusai has his limits.

OEI
…

NISHIMURAYA

It's sad but maybe the time has come.

OEI

What do you mean?

NISHIMURAYA

Why don't you take over, Miss Oei?

OEI

? But I'm a woman.

NISHIMURAYA

You may not be able to succeed him and run the studio, but you can work in his place until you find a successor.

OEI

(Angrily) Are you implying that my father can no longer paint?

NISHIMURAYA

…(His expression says that is exactly what he is thinking)

OEI

I'm disappointed in you, Nishimuraya. It's like you never even knew my father!

NISHIMURAYA

I didn't mean it like that…

OEI

Then what did you mean? No one can replace him!

NISHIMURAYA

But…

OEI

Shut up! No one can capture an image like my father!

NISHIMURAYA

…

Oei kicks everything around her.

OEI

Get out!

NISHIMURAYA

(In shock)…

OEI

I said, get out!

Nishimuraya runs out. Hokusai watches from outside, deep in thought.

HOKUSAI

…

90. Tanehiko's villa / Inner courtyard (A short while later)

Katsuko is arranging flowers in the sitting room.

Tanehiko and Hokusai are talking in the inner courtyard.

HOKUSAI

I've caused you a lot of trouble. It's pitiful.

Tanehiko shakes his head.

TANEHIKO

I'm who I am today because of you, Master Hokusai.

HOKUSAI
…

Hokusai gazes out at the courtyard.

He looks down at his right hand, which shows signs of movement.

HOKUSAI
I was looking forward to illustrating your novels… They're so interesting. Illustrating them made me feel young again.

TANEHIKO
(Flattered)

HOKUSAI
But you can't fool time. Oei scolded me, "When you're 70, you're 70."

TANEHIKO
(Smiles)

HOKUSAI
But Tanehiko, it's not all bad. When I had the stroke, I also had an epiphany. I knew what I wanted to do.

TANEHIKO
?

HOKUSAI
I want to travel for a while.

TANEHIKO
In your condition?

HOKUSAI
Yeah…

TANEHIKO
…

HOKUSAI
There must be things that I can only see now, in my condition.

TANEHIKO
(Considering Hokusai's newfound passion)…

91. Hokusai's house and studio

Compensating for his lame hand, Hokusai opens a wicker trunk and places a few changes of clothes and his sketchbook inside.

Oei looks on, resigned.

OEI
I know I can't stop you.

HOKUSAI
(Moving his hands busily) You're right.

OEI
(Laughing) Don't expect me to see you off.

HOKUSAI
Stop talking and get back to work.

OEI
Where will you stay?

HOKUSAI
I'll find an inn along the way.

OEI
And if you don't?

HOKUSAI
Then I'll sleep by the roadside.

OEI
(Sighs) You're impossible…

Oei gets Koto's memorial tablet and mutters something.

Hokusai wraps the wicker basket in a wrapping cloth and gets up. Oei hands Koto's memorial tablet to Hokusai.

HOKUSAI
…

He takes it without a word and leaves.

92. On the road

Hokusai walks along the road with a walking stick and a basket on his back. The landscape is beautiful.

× × ×

He continues walking…

Hokusai stops to look at a single flower growing on the side of the road. He puts down his basket and takes out his sketchbook, but stops when he holds his brush.

HOKUSAI
…

His hand is still numb. Hokusai puts his sketchbook back and stares at the flower.

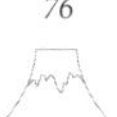

93. On the road (Another day)

Hokusai continues to walk. He sees trees, birds, insects and people at work. He takes in everything.

94. On a road leading to a seashore

Hokusai walks with his stick. The road opens up to the ocean. He sees Mt. Fuji in the distance and listens to the sound of waves.

HOKUSAI
…

× × ×

He sits on the shore. He places Koto's memorial tablet next to him and continues to stare at the ocean.

95. Along a ridge (Early morning)

Hokusai walks in the early morning light. His breath is labored as he navigates the rugged path. The sun rises and the day grows gradually lighter. At the top of the ridge, Hokusai's eyes open wide. He sees Mt. Fuji painted bright red by the sun.

HOKUSAI
(He is moved)…

96. Hokusai's house and studio (A little later)

Hokusai works feverishly on a sketch. He doesn't have complete control of his hand, but it's much improved. Oei and his disciples watch as he paints the same brushstroke repeatedly, as if willing the sensation back into his hand.

OEI
…

97. Tanehiko's villa / Office

A half-written manuscript lays on the desk.

Tanehiko sits on the veranda gazing out at the garden.

TANEHIKO
…

98. Hokusai's house and studio

Hokusai eats a simple meal. His right hand is almost fully recovered. Oei enters, Tanehiko's novel in her hand.

OEI
(Holding it out to Hokusai) Tanehiko's book. "Nise Murasaki Inaka Genji." (Imposter Murasaki and Country Bumpkin Genji)

HOKUSAI
(Takes a quick glance)

OEI
(Worriedly) It's really popular amongst the young kids. They can't print enough of them.

HOKUSAI
(Says casually) That's good.

Oei is wary of his casual response.

OEI
Tanehiko is a samurai, unlike us.

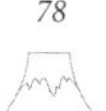

HOKUSAI
There's no reason why a samurai can't write a book when townsfolk can.

OEI
That's the very reason why he'll be punished so severely. Because he's a samurai.

Hokusai stops eating.

HOKUSAI
(Emphatically) Then why don't you go stop him?

OEI
...

HOKUSAI
You think you can? Do you think I'd stop painting because I feared the consequences?

OEI
You and Tanehiko are from different classes.

HOKUSAI
A man with a passion for writing happens to be born a samurai.

OEI
Aren't you worried about Tanehiko?

HOKUSAI
...

Hokusai falls silent for a moment.

HOKUSAI
Tanehiko put everything he wanted to say straight onto the page. That's why it moves the reader. That's what

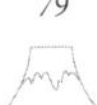

every writer aims for.

OEI
...

HOKUSAI
He can't stop himself. Aren't you the same way?

99. Hokusai's house and studio (Another day)

Hokusai is painting.

100. Hokusai's house and studio (Another day)

A heavy rainfall pummels Hokusai's studio. Hokusai carefully discerns the intensity of his indigo pigment. He pays close attention to the color as Oei and his other disciples, including Kozan, gather around to watch him.

HOKUSAI
…!

Suddenly, he roars, crushes the indigo pigment in his hand and rushes out into the rain! The rainfall echoes, as if to bless him.

101. Hokusai's house and studio (Another day)

Hokusai sits cross-legged and stares at a blank sheet of paper in front of him. He closes his eyes as if to ward off distractions.

HOKUSAI
...

When he finally opens his eyes, he begins to paint quickly with

bold strokes. His eyes take on a lunatic shine.

× × ×

He completes "Thirty-six Views of Mt. Fuji / The Great Wave off Kanagawa."

102. Woodblock carver and printer's studio

Multiple prints of the image are being produced by the woodblock printers.

103. Nishimuraya / Storefront

Customers crowd the store, rushing to buy the prints of the "Thirty-six Views of Mt. Fuji."

104. Nearby houses

"Thirty-six Views of Mt. Fuji." Townsfolk and samurai alike buy the prints and hang them in their homes.

105. Tanehiko's villa and office

Tanehiko holds a print of "Thirty-six Views of Mt. Fuji / The Great Wave off Kanagawa."

TANEHIKO
…

106. Hokusai's house and studio

CAPTION: Chapter IV

There is tension in the air.

Hokusai is in his new studio. It's a simple, undecorated space. Hokusai focuses on his creations along with Oei, Kozan and other disciples. His newest disciple, Kisaburo, moves busily about, assisting the others.

107. Tanehiko's villa

Winter comes to the courtyard. Tanehiko works on his novel in his office while Katsuko arranges flowers. She stands.

KATSUKO
…(As if she wants to say something)

TANEHIKO
(Noticing her)?

He looks up.

KATSUKO
It's nothing.

She shakes her head.

KATSUKO
Please don't work too hard.

She leaves the room.

TANEHIKO
…

108. Meeting Place of the Samurai Union / Interior

It's winter in the courtyard. Tanehiko and Goemon walk down a long corridor that flanks the courtyard.

GOEMON
Lord Takaya, I heard a strange rumor that a novelist named Ryutei Tanehiko is living in your home.

TANEHIKO
…

GOEMON
Have you heard of him?

TANEHIKO
(Hesitantly) No…

GOEMON
I'm relieved to hear it.

TANEHIKO
…

GOEMON
A man of your high morality would never fraternize with someone like him. A man who distributes senseless rubbish.

TANEHIKO
…

GOEMON
Understand?

TANEHIKO
…

He manages to nod, reluctantly.

109. Hokusai's house and studio

Laughter is heard throughout the studio.

The disciples are putting on a show at Kozan's send-off party. He is returning to his hometown.

Hokusai, Oei and Tanehiko laugh and clap as they watch the show.

But a shadow falls over Tanehiko's face every now and then.

HOKUSAI
(Noticing)…

× × ×

The party is in full swing. Kozan breaks from the crowd and comes over to Hokusai.

KOZAN
(Sitting in front of Hokusai) Master, thank you for everything you've done for me.

He bows his head.

HOKUSAI
(Nods)

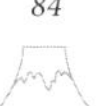

KOZAN
I'm sad to leave this place. Please take care.

HOKUSAI
You, too, Kozan.

KOZAN
(Smiling) I've gotten used to living in Edo. I wonder if I can adjust to life in the countryside of Obuse.

OEI
You can come back any time.

HOKUSAI
(Smiles)

KOZAN
I know it's far, but please come and visit me. There are only mountains, but the food and air taste better there.

Hokusai laughs.

HOKUSAI
I don't know if this body of mine can travel 60 ri. (146 miles or so)

KOZAN
...

HOKUSAI
Write me once in a while.

KOZAN
(Nods)

Kozan returns to the party.

Hokusai is worried about Tanehiko, who looks preoccupied.

He wants to say something, but Tanehiko gets up and leaves. Hokusai follows.

At the party, Kisaburo begins to sing a song about Kozan's hometown, Shinano.

110. Hokusai's house and studio / Garden (Night)

Tanehiko and Hokusai are in the garden. Kisaburo's singing can be heard in the background.

TANEHIKO
It's cold tonight.

HOKUSAI
...

TANEHIKO
Master Hokusai.

HOKUSAI
?

TANEHIKO
Master, could you throw it all away for your art?

HOKUSAI
...

TANEHIKO
Miss Oei, your disciples, everything? ···A meaningless question. I'm sorry.

Hokusai contemplates the meaning of those words.

HOKUSAI
Someday, we'll live in a world where no one can tell

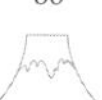

us what to do.

TANEHIKO
…

HOKUSAI
I hope I live to see that day.

TANEHIKO
Me, too.

HOKUSAI
I…only do what I can do. Tanehiko…

Hokusai draws a wave on the ground with his finger.

Tanehiko stands by silently.

111. Hokusai's house and studio (Another day)

Kisaburo is the first to arrive. He starts cleaning.

Hokusai enters and watches him.

HOKUSAI
…

112. Tanehiko's villa / Exterior

Katsuko sees Tanehiko off. He is heading to the Association meeting place. He turns, as if he just remembered something.

TANEHIKO
Katsuko.

KATSUKO
…?

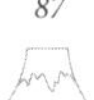

TANEHIKO
Let's go on a trip, once the winter is over.

KATSUKO
On a trip?

TANEHIKO
We'll take our time for a change.

KATSUKO
...

TANEHIKO
And view some flowers along the way.

KATSUKO
I'd love that.

TANEHIKO
(Smiling) I'm off.

Katsuko bows.

113. Hokusai's house and studio

Kisaburo is engrossed in painting. Hokusai looks on.

HOKUSAI
...

114. Meeting place of the Samurai Union (In a dark, closed room)

Tanehiko and Goemon sit opposite each other. Goemon reprimands Tanehiko, his latest novel in front of him.

GOEMON
What is the meaning of this?

TANEHIKO
…

GOEMON
I warned you to kick that parasite out of your home!

TANEHIKO
Parasite…

GOEMON
(Cutting him off) Shut up! You just happened to be housing a thug who was writing trashy novels that offended the shogunate. He caused you so much trouble, you kicked him out. And that's the end of it.

Goemon stands.

TANEHIKO
(Stopping him) A moment. I cannot do such a thing.

GOEMON
Takaya Hikoshiro! You are a samurai, are you not? Do you know what this means for the House of Takaya? Do you?

TANEHIKO
…

GOEMON
Have you lost your mind? Do you mean to destroy your name? Put your family out on the street?

Tanehiko is at a loss for words.

TANEHIKO
…

He questions himself, fists clenched.

Goemon throws the book on the floor.

GOEMON
Rid yourself! Of your foolish demeanor! And your foolish disposition! That's all I have to say.

He makes to leave.

TANEHIKO
Please wait.

Tanehiko stops Goemon and faces him.

TANEHIKO
I…will not. I will not stop writing.

Tanehiko looks directly into Goemon's eyes.

TANEHIKO
I…am Ryutei Tanehiko. I cannot rid myself of that.

Goemon glares at Tanehiko in disgust.

He turns his back on him and leaves.

115. Hokusai's house and studio

Kisaburo is attempting a painting.

HOKUSAI
(Watching him)…

116. Meeting place of the Samurai Union

Tanehiko is surrounded by Goemon and other samurai.

TANEHIKO
…!

117. Hokusai's house and studio

Hokusai watches Kisaburo's brushstrokes.

Loud footsteps approach.

OEI
Father!

Her face is pale.

HOKUSAI
(Turns around)

OEI
It's Tanehiko! Tanehiko…

HOKUSAI
…!!

118. Tanehiko's villa / Front gate

Hokusai and Oei arrive, out of breath.

He bangs on the gate, which is shut tight.

119. Tanehiko's villa / Interior

Tanehiko's body lays on a futon bed. A wooden bucket lies where

his head should be.

Hokusai and Oei sit by his side. Katsuko sits beside them.

KATSUKO
My husband took his own life.

HOKUSAI
...

KATSUKO
They said he died an honorable samurai's death.

HOKUSAI
Mistress Katsuko···

She stands and leaves.

HOKUSAI
...

He removes the cloth covering Tanehiko's face.

OEI
!

She grits her teeth and stifles a cry.

HOKUSAI
...

Hokusai closes his eyes.

120. Hokusai's house and studio (Another day)

It's quiet. There are no disciples in sight. Hokusai is overcome with grief. Yet···he picks up his brush.

Oei enters the room, dejected.

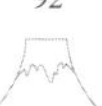

OEI

(Shocked) Father, you're going to paint on such a tragic day?

Hokusai sits in front of a blank sheet of paper.

HOKUSAI

That's exactly why I'll paint.

121. Hokusai's house and studio (After some time)

Hokusai sits in a dim room with a sheet of paper in front of him. He closes his eyes quietly, then opens them…

× × ×

An image of Tanehiko's murder forms in his mind.

He's surrounded by samurai.

He is cornered, yet fights for his life. He is stabbed.

× × ×

Hokusai looks straight ahead.

× × ×

He sees an image of a sword swinging down on Tanehiko's neck.

× × ×

Hokusai closes his eyes.

A frightening painting is left in the room.

"Severed Head"

The final scream of a man whose head has been severed. The man's mouth is wide open, as if trying to say something.

122. Hokusai's house and studio (Another day)

Hokusai sits in front of "Severed Head."

Oei stands behind him, horrified.

OEI
Father, this painting…

HOKUSAI
…

OEI
If the shogunate sees this painting, it'll be your turn next…

HOKUSAI
Oei.

OEI
…

HOKUSAI
I know what kind of man Tanehiko was.

OEI
…

HOKUSAI
He would never commit suicide. They shut him up before he could say what needed to be said.

OEI
Father.

HOKUSAI
…

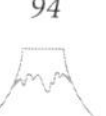

OEI
Let's leave Edo. Please. Listen to me just this once.

HOKUSAI
...

OEI
Father!

She begs him.

HOKUSAI
...

Hokusai stares at "Severed Head."

123. On a perilous mountain road

Oei and Hokusai travel a mountain road. He carries a walking stick and a pack on his back. He chants relentlessly.

124. On a mountain road

They continue to walk.

KOZAN
(Voiceover)
Master Hokusai!

Kozan runs over.

Both Hokusai and Oei are ready to collapse. Their expressions are pained···

125. Obuse / Hekiiken (Atelier) (Another day)

In a dimly lit room, Hokusai is crouched over, painting. He chants, absorbed in painting a picture of a lion warding off evil spirits.

Hokusai's expression is a mixture of madness and sorrow.

126. The atelier / Exterior

Kozan approaches with Oei.

127. The atelier / Interior

Kozan picks up "Severed Head." Hokusai and Oei sit across from him.

KOZAN
Let me hold onto this painting.

HOKUSAI
Thank you.

KOZAN
(Shakes his head)

HOKUSAI
(Looking at the painting) Nothing ever changes.

KOZAN
?

HOKUSAI
I've been alive for almost 90 years, but I see the same things over and over.

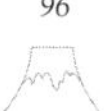

KOZAN
…

After a long pause.

KOZAN
Things will change.

He mutters.

HOKUSAI
?

KOZAN
Someday…

OEI
…

HOKUSAI
…

Hokusai looks down at "Severed Head" then looks up again.

HOKUSAI
Kozan, I have a favor to ask.

KOZAN
What?

HOKUSAI
I want to paint.

KOZAN
…

HOKUSAI
(Thoughtfully) I see words.

Hokusai points to his eyes.

KOZAN
Words?

HOKUSAI
Yes, words. I want to leave them here.

128. A warehouse in Obuse (Some time later)

Hokusai sits in Zen meditation before a huge wooden canvas.

His eyes are closed as he calms his heart.

HOKUSAI
...

Hokusai opens his eyes and stands. He dips a brush in a bucket of paint and begins to paint with powerful strokes. He attacks the work, using every ounce of energy in his old body. His eyes are focused on some other-worldly place. A younger version of Hokusai appears and the two paint together, as if performing a duet in a concert. Their brushes dance, in turn, gracefully and wildly, in the quiet space. Vivid indigo leaps and dances…

× × ×

In the center of an unnamed space are a pair of paintings:

"Angry Waves" – "Masculine Waves" and "Feminine Waves."

HOKUSAI
(Voiceover)
From the age of six, I had the habit of sketching the shapes of things. By the age of 50, I produced many works, but nothing of significance until I reached

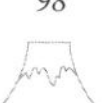

the age of 70. At 73, I began to capture the physical structures of insects, fish and other creatures and understand how plants grow. Surely by the time I'm 80, I'll understand them still better, and by 90, I may grasp the deeper meaning of art. At 100, I will be closer to God and beyond that, I will have reached the stage where every dot and stroke I paint comes alive. May Heaven grant me long life so I can prove this to be true.
("A Hundred Views of Mt. Fuji / Afterword")

THE END

HOKUSAI SCREENWRITER INTERVIEW

Interview with screenwriter Len Kawahara

"The screenwriter creates the blueprint for the movie"

We spoke with Len Kawahara, chief architect and screenwriter of "HOKUSAI." She shared some personal anecdotes and her love for this film.

——What aspect of Katsushika Hokusai did you want to portray most?

How Hokusai lived his life. It's not about the discovery of a natural born genius, but rather a story of how one real and raw human grapples with and overcomes obstacles to rise to heights only Hokusai could have reached.

——How many drafts were there?

13 preliminary drafts and two substantial drafts. So, a total of 15 drafts in the two years leading up to the actual shooting of the film.

——What was the first draft like?

I first wrote scenes which included a huge fire in Edo and a recreation of old Nihombashi Bridge. The producer said, "This will run about 2 billion yen" and nixed it. After that, I struggled not only with the budget but the structure of the story itself. Hokusai thrived even further after turning 70, but if I focused solely on those years, I'd lose the younger audience. I decided it was best to portray his youth as well, but how do I tell a story

that spans a 90-year lifetime? I realized why there were so few movies made about the most famous Japanese artist in the world.

——So what actually happened next?

I returned to the basics and thought, "What would I want to see about Hokusai?" Without a doubt, I'd want to see how he lived his life, but you can't write a story about Hokusai without "The Great Wave." Then the structure of a multi-layered story leading up to the "Wave" came to me.

——And next?

Using a chronology of his life as a guideline, I began researching the intersections of certain people -- who they met and under what circumstances. That's when I discovered that many of Hokusai's illustrated books were published by a bookshop called "Koshodo" owned by Juzaburo Tsutaya. This fact hasn't received much attention, historically. Hokusai had his big breakthrough as an illustrator immediately following Juzaburo's death. I thought, "Is there a story here?" From here, it becomes my work of fiction, but I knew I wanted two turning points: one in his early years and one in his late years. I decided on Hokusai's encounter with Juzaburo for his early years.

——Some unique characters emerge both in his early years and late years.

Yes, Takizawa Bakin, Kitagawa Utamaro and Toshusai Sharaku lived in the same time period as Hokusai, so I wrote about his creative tension with these characters in his early years. In his late years, I introduced Ryutei Tanehiko as a symbol of artistic oppression by the shogunate government to project the theme of the film.

——But Tanehiko isn't really a well-known figure in history.

I didn't know about him either, but through my research,

I learned that he was a best-selling author. So why was he punished? And the year he was punished, Hokusai painted "Severed Head." It was such a gruesome picture, I knew there had to be a story there! That's when I had an epiphany. Could Hokusai's relationship with Tanehiko become the climax of the latter part of the film? But to be honest, Director Hajime Hashimoto wasn't thrilled about the idea of Tanehiko at first.

——Why not?

Tanehiko isn't that famous and he didn't want a sob story climax. But Tanehiko was an "imaginary reality" that I discovered and I didn't want to let him go. Without Tanehiko, Hokusai's story would simply become a success story which would also dilute the existence of Juzaburo in the first half of the film. "Dying as a result of political oppression and punishment" is a theme both Juzaburo and Tanehiko share. Kitagawa Utamaro as well. I thought if I could connect these dots, the story would be very compelling.

——How many drafts did it take to arrive at that conclusion?

About 10. Honestly, it was falling apart until draft 8. I was unable to complete a work of integrity, and we even had to postpone filming once. I continued to write, as if I were standing on the edge of a cliff. My creative juices weren't flowing at all, and I felt like a used-up teabag. When I somehow managed to turn in draft 8 by the deadline, Producer Kenichi Nakayama said, "I think you should give it up."

——What was missing in draft 8?

Draft 8 was just a line-up of all-stars. Nothing that resonated with the soul.

——But you didn't just "give it up" did you?

On the day that I submitted draft 8, I had to go on a business

trip to Finland. I apologized profusely to Producer Nakayama at Narita Airport, but he only said "By the time you come back, we'll have a new screenwriter." It was due to my lack of talent so what could I do? I said, "I understand" but followed up with, "Please give me one more chance."

——*So you rewrote the screenplay in Finland?*

I worked on a new plot on the plane without even taking a break to eat, but when we arrived in Rovaniemi, a city near the North Pole with temperatures of -30℃, my PC froze and stopped working. I thought, "I'm doomed", but I had asked Producer Nakayama for one more chance so I had to do something. I wrote out the plot by hand.

——*How many days did that take you?*

I wrote it in about 6 days. When I returned to Tokyo and typed it into my PC, it came to exactly two hours. Producer Nakayama said "This may work." Maybe writing near the North Pole brought me closer to Hokusai, who named himself after the north star. Or maybe writing the screenplay by hand helped me to convey the vision in my mind more directly onto the page

——*What was the biggest change?*

For instance, there is a scene in Hokusai's early years where he wades into the sea. Up until draft 8, Juzaburo took Hokusai to the ocean in order to help him to "see."

——*And you rewrote it so Hokusai has the epiphany on his own.*

Right. But it wasn't easy. It would seem contrived if Hokusai were to wade into the sea and have a sudden epiphany. To make this discovery himself, he'd have to go through considerable anguish first. So, I added the banquet scene with Sharaku.

——Where Sharaku makes a fool of him.

When someone more talented than you shows you what sets him apart from you, it's devastating. I had flashbacks of the time Producer Nakayama said, "I think you should give it up." (laughs) Not everyone is born or dies a genius, so I was determined to portray the protagonist's anguish very clearly and put him through a lot of suffering. But it's not easy to convey suffering visually -- not from lack of money or status, but from art. Art is subjective, after all. Hokusai was actually very good at painting beautiful women. His drawings were balanced and even more beautiful than Utamaro's. It's a fact that Juzaburo sponsored Utamaro and Sharaku, so he must have invested in Hokusai's unique talent as well. As evidence, Hokusai's masterpiece of beautiful women painted under the pseudonym "Kakou" entitled "Seven Foibles of Young Women: The Telescope" was in fact printed at Juzaburo's Koshodo Bookshop. That's why I added the scene where Juzaburo sees through Hokusai, presents the print and asks him, "Do you paint to compete?" to quash his pride.

——So you added some context to Hokusai's hardships.

The previous drafts didn't have this element, so it was as if a character suddenly appeared, spoke to Hokusai, damaged his pride and then disappeared. Without the back story to put the scene in context, the characters appear flimsy. Similarly, for Tanehiko, I added the scene where he is given a harsh warning by Nagai Goemon at the meeting place for government retainers. As for Juzaburo, I added the fact that he let his younger brother run his family's geisha house business in the red-light district to emphasize his flamboyant Edo lifestyle and character.

——You've been through a lot! So how do you feel now?

When the master of costumes Masae Miyamoto said, "I'm even helping the extras with their kimonos because I love the screenplay" or when Eita Nagayama said, "I want to be in this

film because of the script" or when Hiroshi Abe said, "I'll do it because the screenplay is good" I have to admit I got a little teary-eyed. Also, when comic storyteller Shinosuke Tatekawa told me, "I was so moved by the story, it shook me to my very soul" I felt redeemed! The appraisal convinced me that all the anguish I went through up to draft 8 was worth it.

——*So you're glad you did it?*

Of course. I definitely grew in the process. A screenwriter's job is to create the film's architectural blueprint, which involves many professionals. You can't do it without giving it your all. My sense of purpose as an artist clearly changed after doing "Hokusai."

——*That you have to do your best?*

You can't write a screenplay just by doing your best. Doing your best is a given. Like when I had to write out the screenplay by hand when my PC broke down, you have to have the mental strength to overcome any obstacle, however difficult. Even when you're driven into a corner, you have to find hope and overcome the challenges, one by one. Pour everything you have into the film and do everything you possibly can at the time.

PROFILE

Screenwriter Len Kawahara made her debut as a novelist in 2007 with "Matataki" which was adapted to film in 2010. (Directed by Itsumichi Isomura) Her work spanning several genres includes penning the screenplay for the film "Yomei" (Directed by Jiro Shono), writing the novel "Seinaru Kaibutsutachi" (Holy Monsters), and the non-fiction book "Nine Days - The Fight of Iwate Prefecture's Disaster Countermeasure Headquarters." She also appears as Oei (Hokusai's daughter) in this film.

／HOKUSAI 北斎　シナリオブック

発行　2021年5月13日　初版　第一刷発行

著者　河原れん
発行人　細野義朗
発行所　株式会社 STARDUST HD.
〒150-0021　東京都渋谷区恵比寿西2-3-12
発売元　株式会社 SDP
〒150-0021　東京都渋谷区恵比寿西2-3-3
TEL　03-3464-5972(第三編集部)
TEL　03-5459-8610(営業部)
http://www.stardustpictures.co.jp/

印刷製本　図書印刷株式会社

翻訳　山城美樹
翻訳コーディネート　株式会社アウラ
協力　安村敏信(北斎館)
インタビュー取材・文　イソガイマサト
撮影　濱田利章
デザイン　森田千秋(Q.design)
編集　木村未来(SDP)
編集協力　坂尾昌昭、中尾祐子(GB)
営業　川崎篤、武知秀典(SDP)

ISBN978-4-906953-99-8

Printed in Japan

※本書に掲載しているシナリオは、撮影に使用された「決定稿」です。
演出や編集の意図により、シーンや台詞など、完成した映画とは異なる部分があります。